# MALE SURVIVAL

# MALE SURVIVAL

## MASCULINITY WITHOUT MYTH

**Harvey E. Kaye, M.D.**

GROSSET & DUNLAP
PUBLISHERS

*New York*

FOR
*Diane, the Essensual*
*Stephen, the noblest and most gentle of sons*
*Julie, a daughter of rare wisdom, grace, and radiance*

## Acknowledgments

An author serves as the focal point of countless influences, too numerous to acknowledge individually. To my patients, to my students, and to my psychoanalytic mentors and colleagues I owe inestimable gratitude for providing a rare insight into the depth and infinite variety of human experience. I am particularly appreciative of Miss Susan Rubenstein for her delicate and restraining editorial touch.

# Contents

# MALE
# SURVIVAL

# 1

# The Masculine Mystique

IMAGINE THE DISCOVERY of a new drug, a sovereign remedy with horrendous social import, a nostrum next to which the opiates and psychedelics pale. Omitting its polysyllabic chemical name, I shall refer to it as the Reality Inducer. While opium and heroin lead to a realm of oceanic infantile oblivion, and LSD produces a state of sensate anarchy, my Reality Inducer would create a psychic world devoid of illusion. One who ingests it would see things as they are, rather than as he might wish them to be. It would induce a condition of compassionate detachment in which distortion, myth, and false coloration would be stripped away from reality. Obviously this elixir should not be marketed, lest our social fabric be ripped to shreds. What would happen to the speeches of the politicians, the protestations of lovers, and concepts like honor and heroism, cowardice and martyrdom? How much of our behavior and how many of our beliefs are founded upon individual and collective delusion? But join me in a fanciful dose. Let us relax in its unique effects and contemplate the minds of men.

When Aristotle defined man as a "rational animal," he was being charitable. Men's minds have an outer crust of reason, surrounding a molten core of archaic residues, primordial passions, mythologic themes, and inchoate drives and fantasies. A man's perception of himself and his reality is filtered through and altered by this center. The core is conceptualized as the "Unconscious" by the psychologically-oriented, or as the subcortical centers of the brain and biochemical substrate by the more physiologically-minded. Rage and sexual responses can be localized in areas of the brain beneath the cerebral cortex, the rind of the brain in which the rational processing occurs. However, the manner and type of the reaction are determined by the individual's previous experiences.

The Unconscious, functioning in part as a tape recorder, incorporates within itself previous unremembered experiences, repressed memories, and the unrecognized training to which it has been exposed by parental and other critical figures. These impressions are frequently distorted by inaccuracies, the prejudices and expectations of others, and the exigencies and circumstances of the child's life situation. The Reality Inducer is designed to dispel these distortions and illusions. And nowhere are they more apparent than in the male's conception of his masculinity.

Civilization has created a Masculine Mystique, a complex of quasi-mystical attitudes and expectations surrounding the male in his society. Utilizing parents, peers, and cultural institutions, already unwittingly infected by it, the Mystique softly and subtly insinuates its siren song into the recording apparatus of each man as he develops, luring him from the facts of his maleness to the outer reaches of exaggeration, caricature, and illusion, and finally, at times, to self-destruction. The aura of the Mystique penetrates the essence of a man's existence. Permeating his physical apparatus, his psychological set, and his social interactions, the melody seduces man from what he is, and offers instead a grandiose image all but impossible to attain and still remain human.

At the onset of the birth process, the infant's head descends from the mother's pelvis flexed on its breastbone. Rotating inward, extending, restituting, and finally turning outward, the head greets the outside world, followed by its shoulders and the remainder of its tiny form. The obstetrician, having breathed a sigh of relief that there was no umbilical cord constricting the young neck, confidently grasps the child by its feet, slaps the soles, and is rewarded by the cry which the new mother will find maternally inspiring, and later occasionally maddening. A cursory examination of the pubic area reveals the presence of a penis, and the exhausted mother and nail-biting father are informed that they have a son. From that moment, the cultural indoctrination begins.

The blue blanket, the miniature boxing gloves, the blue Superman tights with accompanying cape, subtly inform this newly-hatched amorphous bit of protoplasm of the great and impossible expectations which constitute the essence of his recently acquired humanity. He is to become the embodiment of heroism and courage, aggressivity and aptitude, an amalgamation of the fantasies of Hemingway and Mailer. The roughhouse play with adults, the injunction that "little boys don't cry," the "did you win?" when he returns home after his first pugilistic encounter with the boy next door, nose bloodied and tears only barely contained: the message is received, the boy is trained to be a "man." Vulnerability is a vice, emotionality is odious, and stoicism connotes strength.

Unconscious conspirators, parents, and society weave the Mystique into the psyche of the developing boy. The seductive promise of limitless potentials proves irresistible.

A spirited marlin rising to the bait, the tad swallows the Neanderthal Ideal, the image of the conquering male, clad in the skins of animals slain in single-handed combat, dragging the woman, his mother or a reasonable facsimile, into his cave. In his dreams and fantasies, he has faced the paternal dragon. Despite his dread of castration or annihilation, he has survived, penis intact, taller and broader in body and spirit. He might now envision himself as a Lancelot who has imaginatively dabbled with Guinevere, while a benign and understanding Arthur has stood patiently by, restrained by the wisdom of a Merlin or a Dr. Spock.

Spurred by the insistent flow of androgens, with its resultant increase in aggressivity and physical growth, a boy's marriage to the Mystique is cemented. Through his rearing, his training in school, and the attitudes of the women he encounters, our young knight is expected and encouraged to further flex his musculature. He must open doors for "the frail sex," offer them his seat on the bus, carry their school books, and pick up the tab at the local soda fountain. Conformity to the Mystique rapidly becomes a measure of manhood, a thermometer of "masculinity." Again, little boys or big men "don't cry." To be a "man" is to be a Gary Cooper, perpetually walking down the street at High Noon, tight-lipped, courageous, determined, and resigned. Four or five guns, malevolently aimed at his guts, are assumed to be the facts of life, to be dealt with by grace and courage. After dealing with the scoundrels, one can always ride off in the buckboard with Grace Kelly, hopefully to a bigger ranch in Monaco.

Following the puberty rite of his particular culture, be it confirmation, bar mitzvah, or a vest impregnated with live wasps placed upon his chest, the boy theoretically enters manhood, with all the "privileges" accorded to the Achiever. Regardless of economic conditions or physical limitations, he is to return with the spoils of the hunt, the fruits of his labors, or suffer the loss of self-esteem. He is to attain status and prestige, and transfer these to his family, in a society which has precious little status and prestige to bestow. Furthermore, our Achiever is expected to assume unlimited responsibilities. In his office, or within the family confines, in the face of unlimited challenges, he is to cope effectively. His legendary sexual prowess is awesome. Expected to produce an erection on demand, and to insistently and everlastingly satisfy his mate, the man must become a sexual athlete. Impotence or infertility equals personal inadequacy. Finally, he must present the appearance of independence in a society predicated on a complex of mutual interdependencies.

Like creativity and rumor, the Masculine Mystique is difficult to delineate. However, recurring themes in dreams, fantasies, and aspirations of men define certain constellations around which it settles. These by no means define its limits, but they will serve as representative illustrations of its manifestations.

## *The Superman Syndrome*

Superman had been imbedded in the recesses of men's minds for thousands of years before he appeared, garbed in red cape and blue leotards, as a comic strip character. Like sugarplums, visions of Superman have danced through male heads, as the superspy, the multibillionaire, the ninety-seven-pound weakling who finally humiliates the two hundred-pound bully. "What would I do if I . . . were a dictator," "had a harem," "were invisible" are all variations on the Superman theme. The image of an indestructible being, all-powerful and victorious, has persisted from the anthropomorphic deities of earlier times through the fantasy figures of today. James Bond, Matt Dillon, and Captain Marvel are the modern-day inheritors of the primitive Superman mantle. 007's gadgetry is but a contemporary mechanized version of the supernatural powers of the Grecian Zeus, the Teutonic Wotan, and the Aztec Quetzalcoatl, and, like Prometheus, he is engaged in the salvation of humankind. Furthermore, he is invincible. You know perfectly well that good old James will emerge victorious at the end. Rather than simply a selfish egocentric deity to be placated, the modern-day Superman has been socialized and made into a pillar of virtue. He is now the defender of women and children, the champion of the weak and the oppressed. Human peccadillos and foibles are beneath him. Gallant, brave, and bold, a Marshal Matt Dillon takes on all comers, but never ends up in the sack with Kitty, again manifesting some superhuman virtue. Even Bond's excursions with women, though not devoid of their pleasurable components, are more a means to an end than an end in themselves. The frank admiration in the woman's eyes is more significant than her orgasm. It is this Superman imago which has been appropriated by the Mystique.

Many men harbor dreams of the superhuman. In the playoff between the real and the ideal, reality ofttimes loses. The thought of limitless capabilities has a transcendent appeal, particularly to men who are overly aware of, or who magnify, their limitations. Physical and sexual inadequacies, social and vocational frailties, wither away when wrapped in the mantle of the Superman. What a lovely hypnogogic fantasy, a daydream one can fall asleep to. Unfortunately, the Superman Syndrome is more than a pleasant reverie. It becomes a totality of expectation, an unconscious goal to strive toward, a reach that inevitably exceeds one's grasp. In contrasting himself to a dimly perceived ideal, the man feels himself less than he should be, a loser. His salvation is to realize the impossibility of his quest and to accept his reality with allowance made for its reasonable improvement. Ah, but how many men can?

The Superman Syndrome is fostered by parents with limitless expectations of their sons. It is furthered by society, through the unreasonable demands which it places upon male shoulders, and by the various media, which project unrealistic images of the masculine prototypes within the culture.

The Syndrome is relished by the advertising industry. Playing upon the viewer's capacity to identify with the Superman of his fantasies, it encourages a man to purchase a particular cologne or razor blade because some baseball or football idol indicates that he uses it. How can a man refuse? Buy them and be transformed. Sports figures are portrayed as Supermen, as long as they bat over .300 or their pass completions exceed 50 percent. I have little doubt that part of the magnetism of the book *The Boys of Summer*, a follow-up on the lives of the old Brooklyn Dodgers, is the presentation of the gods of one's youth as fallible and, too frequently, fallen mortals. What a tragedy! What a relief!!

The boy buys the Syndrome because he has been psychologically primed for it. In the earliest years of his life, he fancied himself omnipotent, and why not! His slightest wish or discomfiture was immediately catered to by the caretakers surrounding him. When he hungered, he cried, and his mother magically appeared to feed him. Were his diapers damp, again he cried, and *violà*, they were changed. Indeed, the world seemed little more than an extension of himself. When he perceived his father as all-powerful, the possibility of a Supermanlike creature existing in reality was reinforced. As the boy develops, his limitations and vulnerability become painfully apparent. Unable to accept the bind of great expectations versus marked limitations, the fantasy of total power, in its varied guises, is utilized to counter his own feelings of inadequacy and vulnerability. The remnants of omnipotency are then projected onto the cultural god-surrogates, but the memories linger on, and slink about his subconscious in the form of Supermaniacal aspirations and fantasies.

We find insecure men comparing themselves to other men they've endowed with superlative qualities, and finding themselves severely wanting by virtue of this unfair and woeful comparison. Fears of latent homosexuality may be entertained to explain their presumptive "failures," or they may hopelessly "cop out," detaching themselves from further striving, and become self-pitying misanthropes or denizens of the hip scene.

Perhaps it is best that Superman remains a fiction. While he may have aided the good citizens of Metropolis, his image has been misused by the Mystique, and has created havoc in many a male ego.

## *The Neanderthal Ideal*

First, a few words of apology to the Neanderthal. Our cultural stereotype portrays this 75,000-year-old Stone Age humanoid as the personification of Brawn: a muscular and hirsute individual who lived by strength alone, dragging his women into caves by their hair, and bashing in his neighbor's skull with his massive club. He may well have been simply an embattled soul, too busy with the essentials of survival to be overly concerned with such superfluities as warfare, rape, and other leisure activities. I see no reason to assume that he was incapable of intelligence, warmth, and affection. But the Mystique feeds on stereotypes, and we must meet it on its own terms.

The Neanderthal Ideal is a reversion to the primitive. The complexities of life, with their tortuous alternatives, are simply solved by the rejection of the rational and the evocation of the physical. When dispute arises, punch if individual, war if national. Consequences be damned; in the end, might has little regard for right. In man's struggle between the sinew and the sensible, the former too frequently emerges on top. The spectre of the male as the physical brute, the ruthless and violent hunter and warrior, emerges as the symbol of "virility."

Bethesda Fountain is a picturesque oasis in the middle of Central Park. On Sundays, New York weather permitting, it attracts hordes of humanity. Expressively attired in what they view as their individual "thing," a multitude of egos enact their conceptualized self-images on this massive stage. Strolling troubadors, strumming guitarists, and bongo bands beating with primitive rhythmicity provide the musical background for the spectacle. The outfits often display the people as they would like to see themselves, and the costumes are varied. One striking motif is the portrayal of brawn: the motorcycle cultists, their jackets unsleeved, exhibit their biceps and deltoids; those decked out in headbands and other Indian paraphernalia recall the "noble savage"; someone uttering the cries of Tarzan as he leaps from vine to bough mimics the caveman. The Neanderthal Ideal comes alive in New York City. Invite the fantasy, it seldom refuses an invitation.

The adulation of the primitive is not confined to the fountain and its visitors, nor to our time and place. The elaboration of the fifteenth- and sixteenth-century codpiece, the padded shoulders of men's jackets, the rugged squared-jaw hero of romantic novels, and the exaggerated simian gait of swaggering adolescents are all extensions of the Neanderthal Ideal. It is also blatantly obvious among the Mister Americas on Muscle Beach.

The Neanderthal Ideal is rooted in our racial and individual histories. During the evolutionary and historical descent of homo sapiens, conditions for survival dictated the development of various qualities in the male that more effectively ensured the survival of the individual and his species. In earlier times, the struggle for mere physical existence placed a premium upon the acquisition of a substantial musculature and supporting skeletal structure to enable the male to hunt, to defend himself and his family from predators, and to aggress when conditions warranted it. While his developing intelligence and tool utilization placed him apart from other animals, the need for physical strength was obvious. The fact that man was approximately 40 percent more powerful physically than woman placed the onus of more arduous muscular labors upon him. Moreover, he was fleeter of foot and more biologically prepared for aggressive behavior than was his mate. When humankind progressed from a nomadic to a more settled existence, it is a fair assumption that the males hewed the forests for timber, while the females prepared the home; and that men killed for skins, while women made the clothing from them. Again, brawn was the sine qua non for the male. This racial heritage has been incorporated in the Neanderthal Ideal.

In a world in which the force necessary to push a button or to press on an accelerator is the requisite strength needed for survival, men still conceive of themselves as muscular madcaps, divinely prescribed to perform miraculous feats of might. Failing this, they fail as men. Boys taunt each other with: "My father can beat up your father." One rarely hears: "My father is nicer than your father." A boy's rough and tumble play is further accentuated by the exaggerated response of adult males in his environment. The capacity to dish it out and to take it is highly praised. And so it goes on, from father to son, and back again.

Presented with guns as playthings, a street lore that sanctifies the "victor," movie and television stars who heartily partake in violence, the attributes of the Neanderthal become further enmeshed in a boy's developing pysche. As he ages, he sees girls ogling shoulder-padded football heroes, and is taught that economic success is predicated on "making it" and riding roughshod over one's competitor. Visions of the caveman reemerge in new contexts. The examples are numerous, but the phantasm remains the same.

Unfortunately, social conditions being what they are, many men are, perforce, addressing themselves once again to their physical prowess and are taking courses in self-defense. Let us hope that the Neanderthal remains no more than a fantasied ideal, rather than the future actuality.

## The Sexual Athlete

The Mystique has encouraged what Freud's biographer, Ernest Jones, referred to as "an unduly phallocentric view" of sexuality in our culture. Man, the primate with the largest penis, is too frequently regarded as a phallus with a body attached as an addendum. Seizing upon the obvious fact that the male has a projecting appendage which must be actively inserted into a female, the Mystique has, at times, deified it, endowed it with magical powers, and expected the man to live up to this glorified exaltation. The male member has consequently been regarded as majestic, while the woman's pudendum, " 1) from the Latin: something to be ashamed of; 2) the external genitals of the female, vulva," has been accorded second-class citizenship. Dreams of towering steeples, racing automobiles, and spaceships blasting off may be penile representations, while purses and holes represent the vagina. The fact that a woman's sexual apparatus has greater orgastic potential than the male's is only now coming to light after thousands of years, and is causing the Mystique considerable concern.

In dreams, the size of a person or object is a frequent connotation of its importance or power to the dreamer. To a child, the size of his parents and other adults is itself indicative of importance and strength. A young boy is awed by the size of his father's phallus, and aspires to reach the same proportions. Similarly, the size of the penis is often equated with a man's virility. The equation states that the massiveness of the penis is in direct proportion to the virility of its possessor. Since all but a very few men have approximately the same erect penile proportions, and many feel their organs to be abnormally small, something is obviously amiss. The problem is that men ofttimes focus their feelings of masculine inadequacy onto their penises. An illustration of this concerns a segment of the homosexual community, the members of which compulsively journey from one public toilet to the next, seeking encounters with a penis larger than their own. They have their trousers specially tailored to accentuate a genital bulge, producing a modernized version of the codpiece of yore. Comparisons are made nightly at homosexual bars and baths. The unconscious wish is to magically incorporate the other man's virility, through fellatio or anal intercourse, or at the least, to neutralize the other male's presumptive superior masculinity. This fruitless and unending quest is both poignant and pointless. They never win: the next one might be bigger.

The male's procreative powers have been so touchy a

subject that the Mystique has averted its eyes, and allowed men to assume that the "infertile couple" was synonymous with "the barren wife." That 30 to 50 percent of infertile couples are childless due to some difficulty in the male is still a well-kept secret. The male takes the credit for the pregnancy. The "proud father" is hailed. (How frequently does one hear of the "proud mother"?) He passes out cigars symbolic of his productive penis. When he doesn't produce, no cigars. Potentates divorce spouses who only give birth to daughters, despite the fact that it is the sperm which determines the sex of the offspring. The infertile male feels unvirile, although the production of sperm and the manufacture of the virilizing testosterone are two separate functions of the testicles. An obstetrical paper on the medical work-up of the infertile male cautions: "The man should be approached with delicacy, interest, and optimism. Careful explanation should be given that the semen quality is in no way related to his ability to perform as a male. Often, telling a man that he is the cause of the infertility problem may be a severe blow to his pride." I have never read so delicate an approach advised in the fertility work-up of a woman. Male fragility in matters procreative is brittle indeed.

It is in the game of Performance that the Mystique reaches its apotheosis and the man is expected to be a Sexual Athlete. The male is conceived as an insatiate satyr, walking about in a state of perpetual erection, able to perform under any and all circumstances, and lecherously enlarging at the drop of a handkerchief or the rise of a hemline. Impotency is not only unthinkable, it is unmentionable, although it is by no means uncommon and appears to be on the increase. Regardless of the level of a woman's arousal and lubricity, the male is expected to satisfy. He must retain his erection and restrain his ejaculation until she attains her requisite degree of orgastic ecstasy. Should he "come" too soon or too late, if he misses that moment of simultaneity, he has played poorly, and may be benched. With women increasingly regarding their climax as a "right," and since the insertor is deemed the responsible agent for the attainment of this right, orgastic failure in a woman is looked upon, by her mate, as a denial by him of her constitutional prerogative. But, pathetically, even if she murmurs, "Honey, it's my fault," he doesn't believe her.

The accomplished Sexual Athlete, the true superstar, is presumed to possess masculine prowess. The Sexual Athlete thus joins the Neanderthal Ideal and the Superman Syndrome in this "Paean to Masculine Perfection," composed and orchestrated by the Mystique.


## The Heroic Imperative

In the preface to *The Lady's Not for Burning*, Christopher Fry quotes a convict who falsely confessed to a murder in February 1947: "In the past I wanted to be hung. It was worthwhile being hung to be a hero, seeing that life was not really worth living." The Mystique, in the form of the Heroic Imperative, has a habit of leading men to their demise.

While the original Greek heroes are regarded as famous dead individuals who became worshipped as quasi-divine, they may have been real or imaginary ancestors, or "faded gods," ancient deities who for some reason were demoted to human status. While the Homeric Hero was a noble and a fighting man, some, like Hector, Achilles, and possibly Hercules, later became objects of worship. Our contemporary heroes may be something less than godlike, but the Mystique has enshrined the heroic as worthy of veneration within the male psyche.

The hero transcends the usual human limitations. He is a representative to men of their archetypal selves, one who epitomizes their grandiose phantasmal images. He is an object upon whom they project their triumphal aspirations, their glorified selves. And woe be to the hero who lets them down! The matador is a case in point. In deliberately defying death in the bullring, he actively embodies the heroic proclivities of the passive spectators in the stands. The *"Olés!"*, the ears and tails awarded for the magnificent performance, are votive offerings accorded not only to the matador, but to the heroic ideal inherent in the primordial egos of his worshippers as well. Should he show timidity, should his spirit flag, he becomes the object of merciless derision and abuse, and must be crucified for it.

Unlike the Superman, the hero must be vulnerable. In danger of defeat, death, or dishonor, he must personally confront a presumptively superior adversary and best him in some form of combat. Despite any duplicity, malevolence, or despicable behavior on the part of his opponent, our paladin must always "play fair" against the odds, and behave in a chivalrous manner. Playing by the Marquis of Queensberry's rules, should his foe lose his saber or pistol, the hero will voluntarily disarm himself and continue the battle hand-to-hand. He is never to knee his enemy's groin or gouge his eyes. Of course, this code shifts the advantage to the enemy, who never indulges in such niceties, but so much the better. While the hero may enjoy the beneficent blessings of divine powers, or have access to supernatural powers and sources, he must never triumph because of them. If Jehovah directed David's slingshot, one's sympathies would shift toward Goliath and David would diminish in stature.

The hero is seldom motivated by personal material gain. Preferably, he is a fighter against evil and injustice in some form. If he rescues a damsel in distress, it must never be for the eventual insertion of his penis within the warm confines of her pulsating vagina, but rather for the defeat of the damnable forces which imperil her. Otherwise, he is just another Sexual Athlete on the make. Should he fight for the return of the ranch for the tax-sheltered millions it produces each year, he becomes merely an acquisitive capitalist. If the battle is joined because the usurper is an exploitative rotter, the hero's subsequent financial windfall is incidental, and his heroic credentials remain untarnished.

Like the matador, his feet firmly implanted in the sand while facing the devastation of the onrushing bull, the hero is fearless. He faces death with equanimity. With his competence and self-sufficiency assumed, stoicism is the order of the day. A display of "feelings" or "softness" is uncharacteristic, for the Heroic Imperative dictates an emotional vacuum, which again raises the hero beyond human expectations. "Men don't cry"—or show fear, or display tenderness. Activism displaces caring for. The heroic stereotype generally speaks in monosyllables, "yep" or "nope." Discourse is diversionary and intellectual, action is all that counts.

Few men are heroes, neither to their valets nor to their families and neighbors. Consequently, the hero is usually a wanderer, one who intrudes into a situation. His background and birth are generally enshrouded in mystery, and his future is symbolized by his riding off into the sun, rising or setting as the case may be. Where does he go next, presumably to perform further feats of heroism? He must ever keep up his employment as a hero; it's part of the contract. This makes it rather rough on the man who opts for the settled family existence, or who attempts to constructively consolidate the social gains of his noble activities.

Above all, the hero is never a coward. The "man's man" never shrinks or cowers. In *Man and Superman*, George Bernard Shaw has Don Juan, the Shavian version of Superman, observe: "He loves to think of himself as bold and bad. He is neither one nor the other; he is only a coward. Call him tyrant, murderer, pirate, bully; and he will adore you, and swagger about with the consciousness of having the blood of the old sea kings in his veins. Call him liar and thief; and he will only take action against you for libel. But call him coward; and he will go mad with rage; he will face death to outface that stinging truth. Man gives every reason for his conduct save one, every plea for his safety save one; and that one is his cowardice. Yet all his civilization is founded on his cowardice, on his abject tameness, which he calls his respectability."

The Mystique has transplanted the Heroic Imperative deep within the male breast. Under its aegis, men have leapt into impossible situations, endangering life and limb in vainglorious attempts to follow its dictates. In combat, in absurd street situations, in their pretenses to their children and sweethearts, men have divested themselves of their rational perspectives in attempts to assay the tests which the Mystique prepares. When faced with guns, knives, superior numbers, or simply their inadequacy in the face of the impossible, the call should be for self-preservation, not heroics. But, as always, the Mystique flays those who do not follow its imperatives, and men do die rather than face the loss of "masculine self-esteem."

## The Achiever Complex

Ever since Eve's fraternization with the serpent and her appetite for apples caused mankind's ouster from Eden, man has had to exert himself in the cause of providing sustenance for his, and his family's, survival. The Mystique, however, is seldom satisfied with the basics. Extrapolating from life's labors, it has devised the concept of the Achiever, the accumulator of status and prestige that rank a man as "worthwhile" or "important," or something other than a wastrel or a bum. No longer is the fact of labor sufficient. The type of work, and its various fringe benefits, provide a seldom-to-be-satiated goal, the nebulous measure of a man. To further complicate this artifact, the Mystique has ordained that not only is a man to be judged by his status accumulation, but his family is similarly to be evaluated by his performance. Temptingly, it whispers: "More, you owe it to yourself. More, you owe it to them."

The scramble for achievement is primarily found in the upwardly mobile middle class. The lowest on the socio-economic scale see the climb as too high, with the odds significantly stacked against them. Those at the top have no appreciable gains to make. But those in the vast middle strive. They catch glimpses of the jackpot in the sky and are the most vulnerable to a fall. Urged on by the work ethic, which trumpets "Work is Beautiful, and the more you work the more Beautiful you become," they strain for the highest house on the hill, the more prestigious job, and the more expensively attired woman. The symbols of achievement become the goals, rather than the enjoyment of their gains.

Men happy with their vocations as teachers are urged to become principals; brilliant medical clinicians and researchers are pushed into the role of departmental administrators; artists become commercial hacks; and contented workers rise to be alienated foremen, neither blue-collar nor management, and under continuous stress. To remain on a comfortable level is seen as somewhat sinful, and those pushed against their will to "advance" too often advance to an unhappy state. They can take solace from their enhanced status or console themselves with that extra martini or two, or three, or four.

Since the Achiever Complex grows fastest in the vocational medium, the other areas of a man's life suffer. The Achiever becomes the tired husband or absentee father. With the work week of a self-employed person averaging some fifty-five hours, moments of leisure are few, and ofttimes are apt to be spoiled by feelings of guilt, since funtime does not feel productive.

The Achiever Complex begins in the cradle and ends in the grave. The competition between mothers as to whose son sat up first, uttered "Mama" earliest, or "really" took those initial few steps is fearsome to behold; and this rivalrous stance is inculcated into their offspring. In kindergarten, the mother explains that "Doing as well as Johnny isn't good enough; you should be the best." The excitement and wonderment of the school experience is of secondary importance compared to the superior grade on a report card. As the boy becomes the man, he is presented with the American Dream of two cars in every garage, and so much the better if one is a Cadillac and the other a Mercedes. He is even urged to contemplate his own death: the type of funeral, the height and decor of the tombstone, or who has the biggest mausoleum. Once again, and for the last time, the question is posed: "How much land does a man need?"

I do not mean to imply that achievement per se is suspect or bad. There is joy in mastery and excitation in expanding one's domain, talents, and capabilities. These are personal additives which broaden the view, scope, and breadth of one's life. But I do inveigh against the obsession with achieving and the compulsion to accumulate status and prestige at the expense of the remainder of one's personality and life. It is this neurotic imbalance, this unconsciously ordained tunnel vision of life, which the Mystique fosters. It will in all likelihood be only partially modified when the American Dream reestablishes its roots in reality.

## The Paradise of the Playboy

The essence of the Playboy lies in his very name. He is neither "Playman," nor "Playmate," nor "Playmaster." He is "Play*boy*"—the puerile prototype, the ever-young, never-responsible child at play. The eternally youthful prince, with a world of females, fun, and games as his domain, the Mystique-infused ideal of every red-blooded American boy. This is "where it's at," what life should be like.

The Playboy is the fantasied prince of each man's childhood, now grown taller and operating in the adult world. He is devastatingly attractive to scores of women, who pantingly stand in line to enroll in his harem. Women are his toys, his playthings. These "playmates," who have apparently cornered the market on massive mammae, are eager and inviting. The Playboy's sexual proclivities and capacities can be equated with those of a rabbit. Hippety-hop, hippety-hop, he leaps and bounds from encounter to encounter. Like the lillies of the fields, he toils not, but oh, how he spins.

His pad is plush and furnished with a plethora of gadgets: hi-fi's, stereos, mood lighting, cameras, and poster art. A carefully stocked bar and wine rack fill his playroom, while motorcycles and sports cars occupy his garage. His life is filled with leisure time, and any idea of a struggle for survival is far beyond his ken. Truly, he is the envy of every man from Beirut, Lebanon, to Bayonne, New Jersey.

The male retains his charter membership as a Playboy as long as he retains his youthful armor and can afford the expense. Where is there to be found an aging, impoverished Playboy? His membership is revoked with age, unless he has accumulated great wealth. In that happy circumstance, he becomes a man of mystery, a "sport," a gay *boulevardier*, or a randy old rascal whose company is courted by the beautiful people. Should his fortunes fail, he becomes a lascivious old lecher and a hanger-on.

The Playboy, as exemplified by the magazine of the same name and others of its genre, happily never *has* to perform. The "playmates," exposing a cascade of pubic hair or a nipple here and there, provide titillation for happy Playboy fantasies. The male reader becomes a voyeur, under no compulsion to demonstrate sexual feats of derring-do. The editorship is seemingly aware of this, and at times tweaks the proverbial noses of its subscribers. A typical cartoon shows a busty damsel and a moustached Playboy in bed. Our heroine speaks: "Well, if that's what you call sowing your wild oats, you've had a crop failure." It's a funny cartoon. The reader intuitively knows that "There but for the Grace of God . . ."

Since the Playboy symbolizes rampant heterosexuality, the homosexual does not fare too well in this milieu. For example, "Playboy's Unabashed Dictionary" defines a "closet queen" as a "male fraud," and a "transvestite" as a "drag addict," displaying a type of cruel intolerance one finds in eleven- or twelve-year-olds.

The delusion fostered by the Mystique is that this

Playboy Paradise is the norm, rather than a never-never or seldom-ever land. For those very few who live in this supposed paradise, life is often more vacuous than exciting. Most metropolitan areas have their groups of single playboys in their late thirties, forties, and fifties. Those I have known or treated were a rather unhappy lot, unable to relate to women over twenty-one years of age since they were still "boys," bored with their swinging existence, and incapable of establishing anything resembling a gut relationship. Yet the Mystique creates the image, and men are dazzled by it. Not achieving this swinging state, despite their other successes, many feel they have missed some boat, a lost youth perhaps, a magical carefree state. Perhaps life offers more pleasures than the fictional paradise of the Playboy. The Mystique makes too many men overlook them.

## The Dominance Drive

The Dominance Drive is one more illustration of the Mystique's perversion of the normal into the grotesque. Given the hierarchical organization displayed within the multitudinous branches of the animal kingdom (i.e., the well-known pecking order), and admitting the evident though currently unmentionable inequalities among the members of the human race, some rank order in the societal structure is unavoidable, and must therefore be considered "natural" to some degree. While this order is not intrinsically predicated on race, religion, sex, or national origin, apparent inequities in human adaptability and capability are undeniable, and consequently eventuate in unequal distribution of power and mastery potential. Less deeply rooted than the biological drives of hunger, thirst, and sex, the human drive toward mastery is nonetheless compelling, and the Mystique has coerced the male into its exaggerated thralldom.

The mastery mode has its genesis early in infancy. Lost and helpless in his initially chaotic universe, the child learns techniques to order and to control it by trial and error. Crying summons aid, subjugation of the anal and urethral sphincter muscles contributes to his sense of autonomy, and developing locomotive abilities enable him to explore, to become familiar with, and to establish some influence over his environment. The child playing peek-a-boo with his mother is indulging in a mastership exercise. By volitionally covering his eyes, opening them, and then repeating the process, he symbolically controls his mother's appearance and her disappearance, thus reducing the anxiety occasioned by her departures. As the child matures, the suzerainty stimulus provides him with greater authority over his surroundings, promoting self-assuredness and feelings of competency, a reduction in anxiety, and a propulsion toward further exploration and development of his potentials. In some respects, the mastery motif resembles Ardrey's "territorial imperative." Holding sway over a situation, a circumstance, or a group establishes a niche of one's own, a bastion of security which one can fall back upon, an inviolate territory. What rational and loving parent would deny his or her offspring its emanciptation through mastery?

But the Mystique is not a benignant parent. Instead of fostering the healthy modicum of mastery necessary for a comfortable existence, it attempts to saddle men with a drive for dominance, an obsession with power. In its more extreme forms, the Dominance Drive is unlimited in scope and is seldom satisfied. Dominance ploys or power plays abound in all areas of the affected man's life—sex, vocation, marriage, recreation, money, etc. Contaminated by the Drive, original purposes and rewards fade, and are replaced with one all-consuming aim, the acquisition of power.

A young man entered psychotherapy complaining of the emptiness and aloneness which pervaded his life. It was soon apparent that his consummate desire to become a millionaire as rapidly as possible had subordinated all his interpersonal relationships to a negligible role. Would he really be satisfied with one million?

"To be honest, no."

"Five?"

"No."

"Ten Million?"

"I know this must sound ridiculous, but I'd go for more."

"What if you finally owned the entire island of Manhattan?"

"This sounds even crazier, but I'd have to keep going."

His father was a tyrant whose sceptre of authority was his checkbook. He talked only of money, punished his wife and children by its withdrawal, exercising power by its use and abuse. His son's recurring fantasy was of stuffing the largest wad of bills attainable down his father's throat. Who could blame him?

Marriages are ruined by monetary power plays. Some husbands attempt to dominate a wife by doling out the dollars as one would to a child, by making her ask for money, by giving a daily "allowance," or by graciously donating or denying as whim dictates. The attendant humiliation and debasement felt by the wife is as distressing as the poor sex life which generally accompanies it. The infantilization which husbands are wont to inflict on their dependent spouses adds imaginative inches to their penises. A mother-child game consists of the mother clapping the child's hands together while she intones: "Clap hands, clap hands, till Daddy comes home, Daddy has money and Mommy has none." With each repetition of the chant, the child is instilled with the power of the buck, and the dominance of the male who controls it. The Mystique's Dominance Drive gains another adherent.

The delights of sexual coupling are often contaminated by misplaced dominance ploys. One spouse, husband or wife, by giving or withholding sex from the partner displays his or her power over the other. The "missionary position," male atop and female beneath, loses its utilitarian sexual function and becomes a dominance symbol. Some men are threatened to the point of erectile incapacity should their mates assume the "superior" position during sexual intercourse, despite the uncomplicated physical fact that many women have a clitoris so situated that it is more easily stimulated by this posture. "Making it with her," "putting the blocks to her," and "laying her" have their power inferences. Too often, sexual stimuli are barely perceived, and are instead submerged in a slew of power fantasies in which the Mystique mutters, "Look how strong and dominant you are," or "You have the power to subdue or hurt, you devil you."

Dominance displays are so rampant in the business world that it would require a Machiavelli to write an appropriate compendium. The key to the Executives' Washroom adds little to a man's urinary comfort, but adds much to his hierarchical rank; a corner office does not materially broaden one's view of the world or enhance one's performance, but it does widen its possessor's range of power.

Under the aegis of the Dominance Drive, the camaraderie of one's fellows becomes transformed into a viciously aggressive tug of war, and man's relationship with woman as well becomes distorted and dehumanized. But the Mystique has absorbed a Nietzschean will to power, and too few men resist it.

## The Myth of Male Superiority

The Mystique, like any superb salesman, mixes its pitches. The Superman Syndrome and the Heroic Imperative are sold softly, but in its propagation of the Myth of Male Superiority, the sell is hard, strident, and simple: The human race is divided into two groups, male and female. The former is the innately superior, and is anatomically designed to rule over the latter. Given this divine ukase, the male is to continually exhibit his pre-eminency, live up to his role, and damned be he who first cries "Hold, enough."

The Myth of Male Superiority is a delusional snare, initially predicated on the possession of a few protruding inches of spongy penile tissue and a somewhat larger physique, which has been ceremoniously sanctified in all cultural institutions, with the possible exception of the obstetrical ward. It reaches its ludicrous extreme in the megalomania of machismo and in the assumption of the universality of penis envy among women.

"Macho," a derivative of the Mexican word for "male," has become synonymous with the grandeur of things masculine, in status, pretension, size, and power. The male displaying machismo becomes a strutting peacock, albeit devoid of the latter's delicacy and finery. The swaggering gait, the gross braggadocio, and the readiness to "fight unto death" present a childlike caricature of penile supremacy. Acting under the tyranny of the testicles, the macho fancies himself a warrior, often armed with knife or gun. Should any insult or innuendo be directed toward him, he is ready to use these penile equivalents for defense. He boasts; he challenges; he preens; he displays. These minor pomposities might be laughable were they confined to display behavior, but machismo has become a way of life, not only in Mexico and other south-of-the-border regions, but also among many street gangs in the United States. Street fighting allows for the display of one's "balls," and a chance to add oak leaf clusters to machismal medallions. Shootings and stabbings thus acquire the aura of normalcy in this jungle of the grotesque.

The depreciation of the female is embedded in the machismic core. Women are deemed inferiors, conquests to be made, laid, and boasted of, except, of course, for one's mother, who is placed on an asexual pedestal. The family constellation often found in the machismo culture is characterized by a relatively detached or absent father and a warm mother-son relationship. A strong emotional dependency upon the mother develops as a consequence. The macho male will fight to the death should her honor be impugned, and he displaces his sexual feelings for her onto other women.

Machomania, rather than representing male superiority, portrays the male at his worst, as little more than a puppet, controlled by that master puppeteer, the Mystique.

Sigmund Freud stands as one of the few authentic geniuses of the past century. His solitary voyage into the then uncharted depths of the mind, and the prodigiousness of his discoveries there, have earned him a permanent place in humankind's Hall of Fame. But being human, Freud was not infallible. As a clinician he was impressed with the material his clients presented. The women who sought his aid were nurtured in an oppressive Victorian-like atmosphere, and were largely suffering from hysteria and pseudo-hysterical illnesses which might be considered schizophrenia today. A deeply rooted envy of the male and his penis was the typical finding in these women of the 1890s and early 1900s. Since Freud was firmly oriented in a biological tradition, he perceived "penis envy" as an inevitable consequence of the genital differences between the sexes and gave insufficient weight to the cultural factors that may have been involved. He went on to conclude that "Anatomy is destiny," with all women fated to strive hopelessly for a penis of their own. The Mystique, never turning down a succulent plum, has heralded this dictum as a scientific verification for its grandiose pretensions. Never mind Freud's writings on men's anxieties, fear of passivity, dread of castration, and unease when confronted with a vagina!

The concept of male "superiority" is not only questionable, but probably untenable. The Mystique, however, is more concerned with impression than with truth. But then, the same can be said of political campaigns, social conventions, and so many other absurdities by which we live.

By this time it should be obvious that the Reality Inducer will reveal a vast variety of syndromes woven by the Mystique to glorify the masculine at the expense of the individual male. The Idolatry of Independence, for example, precludes a man's partaking in the mutuality of assistance which a stable society provides and which is essential for a satisfactory life. The man afflicted with this syndrome will "go it alone." He may be seen at the periphery of any group, opening up to no one, and existing in a not-so-splendid isolation. The Portentous Patriarch will project a prophetic and fearsome image, the Moses of Michelangelo, replete with a ponderous authority and a paucity of humanity—and on and on it goes.

Since the Reality Inducer is not for sale, I would

recommend the following. Periodically pretend you are a visiting alien and read the local newspaper with the presumed dispassionate detachment of a foreigner. It provides an unparalled sense of perspective. On any page one finds the cultural assumptions, the loaded clichés and phraseology, all highlighting the distortions and biases of which we are usually unaware. What would you tell the folks back home? What are we like? What are our tribal customs, collective beliefs, and illusions? The basic idea is to put distance between your assumptions and your reality. Detachment invites perspective; and perspective is conducive to a more realistic appraisal of what's really going on in your life.

Although the Masculine Mystique deals with distortions of reality, it must eventually come face-to-face with the facts of men's lives. Let us see how it fares.

# 2

# The Male in the Masculinity Maze

*His life was gentle, and the elements*
*So mix'd in him, that Nature might stand up*
*And say to all the world, "This was a man."*
WILLIAM SHAKESPEARE

COUNTLESS MEN have needlessly died trying to live up to their masculine ideal; children playing "chicken," young men in battle, old men in the arms of their mistresses. Others have shackled themselves to demanding careers or abnegated their humanity in a relentless drive for power in attempts to validate their virility. What are they demonstrating? What are they proving? In the quest for manhood, what is the Holy Grail? Surely, there is more to masculinity than muscles and genitals. In our quantified society, what is the measure of a man?

A satisfying definition of "maleness" or "masculinity" has yet to be delineated. Webster's New World Dictionary of the American Language defines "male" as "designating or of the sex that fertilizes the ovum of the female and begets offspring: opposed to female," as if his reproductive function was his sole distinguishing hallmark.

"Masculine" connotes: "1) male, of men or boys; 2) having qualities regarded as characteristic of men and boys, as strength, vigor, boldness, etc.; manly, virile; 3) suitable to or characteristic of a man," emphasizing the muscular. Feminine qualities are defined as "gentleness, weakness, delicacy, modesty, etc.; womanly." Questions arise. Is an infertile male lacking in maleness? Is the homosexual or the misogynous man deficient in his masculinity? Are large muscles and headstrong rashness the mark of a man? Are gentleness and modesty unmanly? Are all intellectual snobs effete? These definitions no more delineate the male than Kate Millett's description of femininity as "a delight in docility and masculine dominance" demarcates the female. Chaos is added to confusion. Perhaps maleness or masculinity, the societal manifestation and appreciation of maleness, is a phenomenon composed of three derivative elements: Biological, Psychological, and Social, and so its definition is, like Gaul, divided into three parts.

The Biological encompasses the possession of the requisite sexual organs found in the male of the species, the penis and the testicles. Add the secondary sexual characteristics, the typical male hair distribution, a lower-pitched voice than the female's, a skeletal structure with a more shallow and narrower pelvis, heavier bone structure, etc., with appropriate allowances made for the age of the man. The more subliminal factors, such as odor and gait, are subtle undertones.

The Psychological includes a man's sense of himself as a member of the male sex, identifying with other men of other places and other times. It incorporates a natural acceptance of his manhood, coupled with the capacity to project this feeling about himself to other people. Add some positive relatedness to the female sex, real or fantasized.

The Societal involves being perceived as distinctly male by other members of society, both male and female. The man's partaking, to some reasonable extent, in the varied activities and roles normative for the male in his particular society would be subsumed. This Societal aspect is flexible in a changeable social milieu. It can be generally assessed, however, at a particular point in time. For example, physical strength and muscular prowess may have been a more essential component of masculinity in the nineteenth century than it is in the 1970s.

Utilizing this definition as a conceptual framework, let us add the body to the skeleton.

## The Biological Base of Masculinity

The fundamental similarities and differences between men and women are represented in the chromosomal structure of every cell in the human body. Of the forty-six chromosomes in each cellular nucleus, the twenty-two pairs of autosomes, the body chromosomes, are alike in both males and females. When the Frenchman shouts *Vive la différence*, he is referring to only one of the two sexual chromosomes in each nucleus. A woman possesses two X chromosomes, while a man has one X and one Y chromosome. Thus, from the genetic standpoint, man and woman are 98 percent alike. The 2 percent differential between the sexes has neither a positive nor a negative connotation. The Y chromosome is the hallmark and starting point of maleness, for it programs the anatomy and the endocrine system of the male embryo.

The primary function of the Y chromosome appears to be the inducement of the primitive embryonal gonads to develop into testes rather than ovaries. Its absence will result in the development of ovaries, with femaleness the consequence. Once the embryo develops the testes, during the sixth to twelfth week of intrauterine life, the Y chromosome's initiatory role is finished and the developing gonad now takes over this delicate developmental mosaic. Tiny testicles begin to produce minuscule doses of androgens, the male sex hormones. "Hormone" is derived from the Greek word *hormon*, meaning to stimulate or excite. They are chemical substances produced in various glands and organs of the body, which, when released into the bloodstream, exert their stimulatory or occasionally inhibitory effects on distant "target organs" elsewhere in the body. Thus the Thyroid Stimulating Hormone produced by the pituitary gland stimulates the thyroid gland to produce its hormones and regulates the body metabolism. In like fashion, the primitive testicle produces its androgens, primarily testosterone, which masculinize the fetus. Under the influence of testosterone and an associated hormone which inhibits development of the female reproductive apparatus, a penis rather than a clitoris develops from the primordial genital tubercle, and a scrotum develops in lieu of the vaginal lips. Beyond these evident and elemental anatomical results, testosterone floods the developing brain, and specifically "masculinizes" it. At the base of the brain, just above the pituitary gland, lies a constellation of critical brain cells known as the hypothalamus. Only .3 percent of the total brain weight, it is involved in such crucial bodily processes as temperature regulation, rage and hunger responses, sexual behavior, and other essentials. Instead of the cyclical production of the two female sex hormones, estrogen and progesterone, the masculinized hypothalamus is involved, via the pituitary, in the steady stimulation of the testicle to produce a constant testosterone supply to the male, and controls the characteristic male behavior during sexual activity. An area of the thalamus, just above the hypothalamus, is converted into the mediator of the male erection. In close proximity to these areas lie the centers for aggression, oral activities, and smell, all of which are involved in sexual responses. In all likelihood, excitation of the cells in one area spills over to those adjacent, eventuating in variations of sexual activities, thus producing a mix of several ingredients in the sexual stew.

The absence of the Y chromosome results in femaleness. The X chromosome, without the Y's introduction of androgens, automatically results in the evolution of ovaries with their production of female sex hormones. The female external sexual apparatus, the clitoris and vagina, and the internal reproductive organs, the uterus and fallopian tubes, differentiate when androgens are not added to the milieu. When animals have their gonads surgically extirpated at an early critical period in their embryonic development, anatomic females result, regardless of their chromosomal structure. Variations in this genetic structure produce some variation in the "femaleness" of the woman. A woman with only one X, but no Y, might show an absence of ovarian tissue, with a consequent lack of estrogen. She would then exhibit absence of breast enlargement, a small uterus, and minimal amounts of pubic hair, but she would still be unquestionably female. To date, no human male has survived with only one Y and no X chromosome. It would therefore appear that nature is geared toward the production of females, unless androgens interfere.

While testosterone is the hormone of maleness, the two primary sex hormones in women are estrogen and progesterone, both manufactured by the ovary. Estrogen induces the enlargement of the breasts, the functional responsivity of the vagina, the characteristic hair and subcutaneous fat distribution, etc. In brief, estrogen is involved in those external features which label an individual a female. Progesterone, manufactured by the ovary after each monthly ovulation, prepares the various organs to receive and nurture a fertilized egg and to support the ensuing pregnancy. It stimulates the milk-secreting glands in the breasts to enlarge, resulting in the breast engorgement many women feel prior to their menses, and effectuates changes in the lining of the uterus, enabling the egg to firmly implant in the uterine wall. Estrogen is the dominant hormone of the first half of the menstrual cycle, while progesterone becomes increasingly dominant in the second half, after ovulation has occurred.

Some observers have noted emotional fluctuations in women, perhaps related to their hormonal periodicity. Women's dreams have more active components during the first half of their cycle, and more receptive elements in the second half. Women run a greater risk of suicide in the latter half of their cycle and menstruating women often use violent methods of suicide (for example, 95 percent of females who burned themselves to death were menstruating at the time). The increased sexual interest most women feel during the middle of their cycle is probably a manifestation of hormonal fluctuation, while the male, with his steady hormonal flow, is more constant in the levels of his sexual interest.

Testosterone appears to be the major hormonal factor influencing the strength of the sexual drive, even in women. Lying atop each kidney are the adrenal glands, which manufacture adrenalin and a host of steroid hormones, which regulate sugar levels, mineral and salt utilization, and a myriad of other stress functions. Among the steroids produced are small amounts of testosterone and estrogen in both men and women. Women who have had their adrenal glands surgically removed experience a marked diminution in their sexual drive. Women who have received testosterone injections, for example, in the treatment of cancer of the breast, frequently experience a dramatic upsurge in their sexual interest and drives. It appears to increase the blood supply to, and the sensitivity of, the clitoris. Ergo, testosterone is one of the few known aphrodisiacs. But alas, what nature giveth, nature taketh away, for excess amounts of androgens masculinize a woman, unfortunately negating the utility of testosterone in this area. Testosterone seems to lend immediacy and activity to the sexual drive, which may account for the "Wham, bam, thank you, M'am" component of the male's sexual activity, while the woman, less influenced by it, is more leisurely paced sexually, and is also longer lasting in her erotic activities.

Despite the assertions of some feminist writers that psychosexual personality is exclusively a postnatal and learned phenomenon, there is a rapidly developing body of knowledge to the contrary, indicative of psychosexual predisposition existing either in utero, or at least prior to the introduction of any form of social conditioning. Little girls differ from little boys, not only by virtue of their vaginas, but by inborn psychobiological proclivities as well.

Aggressivity, a presumptive male characteristic, is thought to be simply the result of environmental conditioning by these authors. While our culture obviously increases the level and forms of aggressivity, it is highly probable that the presence of the Y chromosome has some linkage to aggressive behavior. Men with an XYY chromosomal pattern, the possessors of an extra Y, seem more prone to aggress. Investigations of men in prisons reveal a higher incidence of the extra Y than one finds in an average male population. Infant male chimpanzees are more aggressive and more initiatory in their play than female chimps, who appear more adept with their hands and try to communicate more with each other. Standing across a room, one should be able to distinguish a cage of infant female chimps from a cage of infant male chimps by their play behavior. Furthermore, if a female monkey, pregnant with a female fetus, is injected with testosterone at a particular stage in the gestation period, a biologically female infant will emerge, but one who engages in the rough-and-tumble play characteristic of the male. While it is admittedly questionable to extrapolate directly from primate to human, it would be even more foolhardy to evade the probable inferences. If one carefully observes the behavior of human infants, let's say below the age of two, it is difficult not to be reminded of early primate behavior. This is *not* to say that sexual role and behavior is *only* a chemical derivative. But there are distinctive psychosexual differences between the male and the female which simply cannot be dismissed as merely societal indoctrination, although the precise chemistries and neuroanatomical connections have yet to be delineated. The expression of these differences is involved in the biological aspect of maleness and masculinity. The biological maturation of the fetus is followed by, and interlaced with, the psychological adaptation of the child to his gender.

## The Psychological Factor

A sine qua non of masculinity involves a man's sense of himself as the male of the species, with a positive reaction to the fact of his maleness. He "knows" that he is the male in his society, and rather likes the idea.

The "core gender identity," a firmly fixed conviction that "I am a male" or "I am a female," is ineradicably set before the third year of life. In all likelihood, it is the consequence of some form of human imprinting, the fixation of a behavior pattern in an early formative period. If, through parental error or anatomical abnormality, a boy is subsequently found to be biologically female, this conviction of maleness is unalterable after the third year of life. Although biologically female, he should continue to be raised as a male if the error is found after his third birthday. With a firmly fixed core gender identity, the young boy moves on to develop his "core gender role," described by the Hampsons as: "All those things that a person says and does to disclose himself or herself as having the status of a boy or man, girl or woman, respectively. It includes, but is not restricted to, sexuality in the form of eroticism. Gender role is appraised in relation to the following: general mannerisms, deportment, and demeanor; play preferences and recreational interests; spontaneous topics of talk in unprompted conversation and casual comment; content of dreams, daydreaming and fantasies, replies to oblique inquiries and projective tests; evidence of erotic practice and finally, the person's own replies to direct inquiry."

Some investigators, such as Dr. Robert J. Stoller, of the Gender Identity Research Clinic of the UCLA Medical Center, believe that many cases of sexual confusion such as transsexualism (a man who feels that he is actually a female entrapped within a male body, or vice versa) occur when a sufficiently strong core gender identity has not been established.

Inherent in a positive acceptance of one's maleness, a feeling of comfort with one's genitals is included. It is not uncommon to find a man unable to urinate in a public men's room due to feelings of inadequacy about his penis. Many men feel that their penis is "too small." In actuality, significant differences in size of the erect penis are rare and inconsequential. Regardless of the size of the flaccid (nonerect) penis, most erect penises stand equally tall for all practical purposes. Similarly, there is no relation between a man's physique, large or short, and the size of his penis. A man comfortable with his maleness is unconcerned with genital gigantism. In a similar vein, the woman's "cunt hatred" of which Germaine Greer writes is symptomatic of an impairment in a woman's femininity. An aversion to any normal part of one's anatomy is pathologic, until proven otherwise. Ensconced in his masculinity, a man instinctively develops a capacity to project what Saul Bellow refers to as a "message of gender." One need not be a muscle-bound Mr. America nor a cigarette-smoking cowboy to have people, both male and female, think: "There, by God, goes a man." Just as a "natural" athlete impresses us with his competence by his ease of gesture, a maximum of accomplishment with a minimum of effort, the comfortable male radiates the mannerisms, tones, and behavior that one associates with the male gender.

Lionel Tiger, in his book, *Men in Groups*, discusses what he refers to as the "bonding instinct" inherent in the male. Like Kate Millett, I question the instinctual basis predicated by Tiger, but, historically, there has been an obvious element of kinship among men within particular social groups. One assumes that this has reinforced their masculine identities, like the boys getting together at the local tavern for a draught of good ole Brand X beer. A man will empathize more easily with Marc Antony than with Cleopatra, and will more readily suffer with Socrates than listen to Xantippe's complaints against him.

Some institutionalized form of male-female relatedness exists in all societies, monkey, ape, and human. After all, masculinity and femininity are complementary, even though the balance may sometimes be inequitable and repressive. One must come to terms with the opposite gender. In his formative years, a boy develops a concept of himself vis-à-vis the opposite sex. In our culture, his primary lesson is learned from his give-and-take with his mother or mother-surrogates. During this interaction, he incorporates a lifelong impression of how women feel toward him, and vice versa. An affectionate and interested mother bequeaths to her son a positive expectation from women, a feeling of being important and worthwhile. By acting in accordance with this expectation as he develops, he is likely to obtain precisely this response from the future women in his life. During this interplay, his father hopefully will serve as an approving, non-threatening, solid masculine model who reinforces the child's aspirations both as a male and as a human being.

During the period of life between the fourth and eighth year, often called the Oedipal Phase, a boy becomes to some degree "erotically" attached to his mother and simultaneously regards his father as a rival. Feelings of sensuality referential to the female are developed and dealt with. If his mother responds to him positively, without overdoing it, and his father does not regard it as too personally threatening, the boy is imbued with an assertive component to his sexuality, thus extending and amplifying his gender role. A negative and destructive maternal relationship, on the other hand, will raise doubts and anxieties in the boy's future dealings with women. An overly demanding and rejecting mother can easily induce a sense of inadequacy in the boy. A detached and hostile father is frequently found in families of homosexual men. The young boy simply is not equipped to deal with a superabundance of maternal sexuality and paternal threat.

I have been impressed with a seeming lack in projection of gender in men who were reared, during their formative years, in homes devoid of interested females.

As adults, they are often basically indifferent or hostile to women as human beings, and, despite the fact that some marry, they expect little from women as people, as lovers, as wives, and as mothers to their children.

Misogynists have a flaw in their masculinity. That portion of a man's personality which proclaims: "You are a woman, and an attraction exists between us because I am a man," is not apparent. The woman hater denies the female, and consequently negates the masculine counterpart within himself. A healthy young boy, equipped with the biological and psychological necessities of malehood, brings these attributes into play within the cultural area of the masculine mosaic.

## The Societal Sector

The social component of masculinity is partially predicated on a male's adherence to some norms of behavior within his society, and a reliance on these norms to indicate the range of roles he may comfortably play. This by no means describes what should be, but concentrates rather on what currently is. I know of no past or present social grouping in which there has been no significant difference between male and female dress, behavior, activities, or status. These aspects are the most fluid, most variable, and most exclusively socially indoctrinated aspects of masculinity. They change with time, culture, and mores, being least static in periods of rapid cultural change, such as we are currently experiencing. While one can discuss generally accepted concepts of masculinity from a historical vantage point, it is probably impossible for anyone to accurately and specifically delineate the male social role at the time in which he lives, especially if conditions are in a state of flux. The best aspiration for an observer is to impart a general assessment of the male's role in a reasonably objective fashion.

Perhaps the most historically representative, and certainly one of the earliest philosophical prototypes, of masculinity and femininity was devised in China some three thousand years ago with the formulation of the principles of Yang and Yin. The Tao, the rhythm and sense of the universe, encompassed these two elemental forces. Yang, the male principle, had the attributes of activity, positivism, production, light, and life. Yin, the female principle, was passive, negative, earthy rather than spiritual, dark, cold, and dead. The Tao contained these two elements in a constant dynamic equilibrium, with one complementing the other. With occasional exceptions, the extension of these principles has persisted in varied cultural mystiques to the present day. The active and productive male, the passive female; the enlightened man, the silly woman; the spiritually uplifted male, the priest, Jesus, versus the earthy woman with the darkness of her womb, etc., can all be readily viewed within the Yang-Yin framework. How much more deeply ingrained are these atavistic concepts than are the rags and snails and puppy dog tails as the formative components of young males, and the sugar and spice and everything nice as the constituents of little girls. Throughout recorded history, the male role has been the aggressive, the active doer of deeds. The woman has been passive, attached to the home and hearth, *Kinder, Küche, Kirche*, the consort and simultaneously the opponent of the Yang. In this most balanced of philosophical constructs, the balance always seemed to swing toward Yang, with Yin relegated to a supportive and minor role. One can always counter this by mentioning the Virgin Mary, the Amazons, or Joan of Arc, but they are the rare exception, and Joan was burned for it. The woman's role was still subsidiary and circumscribed, and any deviations were ipso facto excluded from the boundaries of femininity.

However, as Tennyson observed, "The old order changeth, yielding place to new. And God fulfills Himself in many ways." One can only hope that if God is presently fulfilling himself, he has a reasonably good idea of what he is doing. With the maturation of social consciousness in our society, class distinctions are losing their force, and the class "female" is asserting itself, demanding more equitable treatment, and getting it. Men find themselves currently at sea, seeking an adequate lodestar to follow, a guiding principle to which they may hitch their masculine identities.

For the forseeable future, men may be expected to gravitate toward those social roles in which they are most likely to excel. While no one is presently in a position to definitively define these areas, we do have some helpful hints.

Erik Erikson's classic experiment is a case in point. One hundred and fifty school-age boys and one hundred and fifty school-age girls were presented with a group of dolls, of both child and adult varieties, animals, furniture, toy automobiles, and blocks. They were then asked to construct "an exciting scene from an imaginary moving picture." The girls' creations were primarily representations of "inner space." They concentrated on the interiors of houses, or enclosed their buildings with doll figures situated within the walls. The atmosphere was relatively peaceful, although intrusions by dangerous men and animals were not uncommon. The boys, on the other hand, built high towers, walls with obvious protusions, and concentrated on external scenes, with moving automobiles and animals. They produced frequent automobile accidents, robberies with the thief being apprehended, collapsing buildings, and ruins. These ruins were found exclusively in the boys' constructions. Whether these creations are representative of the "somatic" or bodily configuration of the individual girl or boy is questionable. They may portray castration anxiety in boys, with the expectation of being caught and "ruined," or they may have merely expressed the social conditioning to which these youngsters had already been exposed. These questions are, for the moment, beside the point. This experiment does, at the least, represent interest and attitudinal differences presently within our culture that indicate decided predilections in social role.

Other studies reveal no significant differences in intelligence between men and women. There appears to be a greater verbal fluency in girls, a more rapid rate of intellectual and emotional development up to the start of their college years, when male-female differentials begin to equalize.

Talcott Parsons, a Harvard University sociologist and an acknowledged leader of the functionalist school of sociology, conceptualized the masculine role as "instrumental," with the associated traits of aggressiveness, tenacity, curiosity, ambition, planning, responsibility, originality, and self-confidence. He characterized the feminine role as essentially "expressive," as evidenced by affection, sympathy, obedience, cheerfulness, kindliness, and friendliness to both adults and children. He also added negativity and jealousy, which sounds suspiciously like the Yin. Once again, man is seen as the active instrumental agent, while the woman is perceived as the fountain of emotionality, the sentinel of the senses.

While these works may be somewhat dated, and their interpretations open to some argument, they do express areas of interest and commitment to which the majority of men respond. They broadly portray how men view themselves, how they are perceived within our culture, and are consequently elemental in the social component of masculinity.

It is commonplace for a psychiatrist to treat men and women convinced that they are "latently homosexual." Men may feel they have failed as "men" by not emerging as champions in our competitive business world, or women may be unable to resolve their desire to be sexually expressive with their conviction that a "woman" must be passive to be feminine. Some, unable to grasp a cohesive sense of their own masculinity or femininity in the face of ill-defined or caricatured cultural impressions, deny any differences. And so we ogle at the abnegation of sexual roles; we titter at Unisex.

A current story making the rounds concerns a young couple in identical outfits and hair styles, with identical facial expressions, who enter a physician's consultation room for a premarital examination. After a few moments of bewilderment, the doctor turns to them and asks: "All right, I give up. Which one has the menstrual cycle?" "I don't know about the menstrual cycle," replies one, "but I've got a Honda."

There is a pathetic quality to the tale. The confusion, the escape into ignorant oblivion, the meager identification predicated upon the possession of a "male" symbol, the motorcycle, sadly exemplify the devastation of the sexual egos of our future citizenry. There is an apparent need for a definition and reaffirmation of both masculinity and femininity in our culture.

Since our subject is Adam, one might construct an admittedly artificial "Masculinity Index," extrapolated from the previous discussion. Its purpose is not to tag or to label, but rather to provide the questioning male with something more concrete by which he might gauge that most elusive of qualities, his masculinity.

## The Masculinity Index

Consider a theoretical spectrum, ranging from a male devoid of all masculinity to the Superman. Please note that the spectrum is *not* from masculinity at one end to femininity at the other. A male is a male, regardless of how masculine he may appear, and will automatically turn toward the door marked "Gents" rather than toward the "Powder Room." However, some men obviously exude more "masculinity" than others. The scale is constructed from the three attributes previously elaborated (Biological, Psychological, and Societal), and the personal weighting may vary with a man's age and his life circumstances.

I. *The Biological*
1. Possession of the requisite male genital apparatus
2. Possession of the appropriate secondary sexual characteristics of the male

   This would include a lower-pitched voice, an angular rather than a curvaceous bodily outline, the male hair distribution, etc. The muscles need not be mammoth, nor the voice deep and sonorous, for we are dealing with the average rather than the exceptional.

II. *The Psychological*
1. A sense of comfortably belonging to the male sex including:
   a. Core gender identity
   b. Comfort with one's gender role
   c. A happy acceptance of one's sexual apparatus as normal
2. The capacity to project the above

3. A positive acceptance of one's malehood, as evidenced by dreams, daydreams, and fantasies
4. Identification with other men
5. Finding women generally attractive
6. The feeling that one has some attractiveness to women

III. *The Societal*
1. Being viewed by others in the society as securely ensconced in the male segment of the culture
2. Society's positive reaction to the male's projection of gender
3. A reasonable degree of partaking in the society's gender norms
   This would include mannerisms, deportment, interests, vocational and avocational preferences.
4. Anything that delineates a man as individual or unique, without detracting from him as a person
   In accentuating him as a distinctive human being, his other assets are consequently highlighted and increasingly appreciated. The stamp of uniqueness has a transcendent appeal, which places one apart from others and accentuates other assets.

While this system is clearly arbitrary, it serves to delineate "where one stands" in the male spectrum. It should, in fact, be modified to conform to the realities of one's present situation. Thus the Biological and Psychological should be endowed with greater weight in the preteen and teen years, before the boy has had the opportunity to develop the Societal elements to their fullest extent. The older, or aging, man should have sufficiently developed the Psychological and Societal so that his sagging musculature and diminished energy reserves will be more than compensated for. A man who has had surgical castration for prostatic cancer would still feel quite masculine, relying more on a well-developed sense of his manhood in the Psychological and Societal areas. Masculinity, after all, is a totality, and I can think of numerous men, either advanced in years or suffering from some physical infirmity, who exude it to a greater degree than their younger or healthier counterparts.

It should be apparent that there is no passing or failing point in this index. I have never seen a man who is just biologically male, with no other evidence of masculinity discernible, nor have I ever known a true Superman. No one in our complex culture can possibly develop perfectly in all areas. A man who exclusively relies on rugged good looks or muscular physique (the Biological) may fail to develop the Psychological or the Societal. The "professional" male, the doctor, lawyer, or Indian chief, ofttimes is so dependent on the Societal that his Biological and Psychological areas suffer. The vast majority of men will find enough of themselves in this index. Those who still harbor serious questions about their presumptive inadequacy might be well advised to seek a professional consultation.

# 3

# Man's Wonderful Workaday World

A SPECTACULAR ASTRAL EXPLOSION, one monumental miscalculation and the Earth was born. Chaos, cataclysm, fire, and brimstone reigned until, the elements exhausted, quiet descended. The primordial slime set, and the volcanic ooze slithered back into the bowels of the earth. The vaporous mists, writhing and consolidating, ascended, vaulting the Earth in a panoply of incandescent clouds. The rains washed the land and gave rise to the seas. Mother Nature, now liberated from the prison of an inimical planet, borrowed a pinch of lightning from Heaven, added it to a stew of oceanic amino acids, and created life.

First the algae and the amebae, the plankton and the protozoa, then the fishes, reptiles, and dinosaurs; some recipes worked while others were locked away in eternal evolutionary file cabinets, never to be reopened. The final dish, the ultimate in design, dramatically culminated in the creation of Woman, the "first sex," in Mother Nature's own image. In a burst of maternal ebullience, women were endowed with the Earth, with all its proliferating blessings. The fertile plains, the kaleidoscopic foliage, the fruits of the trees, the songfests of the birds, all theirs! The primeval primogenitors of the human race, Daughters of Nature, the planet belonged to them!

Ecstatic in their newly found domain, women formally celebrated their uniquely acquired state with the organization and first meeting of P.A.W. (Prehistoric Alliance of Women). Though naked, these procreators of humanity were not naive. The primary item on the agenda was the issue of continuing their survival in the happiest of habitudes. Blessed with Mother Nature's foresight, they perceived the evident necessity for the creation of a "Provider," a creature to bear the brunt of the heavy work, the abundance of onerous responsibilities, the monetary concerns, the pressures of time, deadlines, worries, commuting, and the assembling of fix-it-yourself toys.

The more pragmatic of the celebrators anticipated certain difficulties, however. How were they to keep the Provider in perpetual servitude and yet motivated to perform its assigned tasks? An ad hoc committee was appointed, and after much discussion in the local sylvan glen, reported its deliberations. The problem had proven simpler than at first conceived. Grant the Provider a penis to glorify (and to fertilize the female's eggs), a more massive physique and larger muscles to feel stronger and more powerful (and to do the heavy work), and a Masculine Mystique to live by. The proposal for the creation of the Provider was then presented as a non-negotiable demand to Mother Nature. Her capitulation was a happy one, with amnesty assured to all demonstrators. The Provider was instantly created from a pubic hair, and was henceforth referred to as "less-than-woman," or simply "Man." With the formulation of this Grand Matriarchal Scheme, the meeting was adjourned.

Eons elapsed. The minutes of the first meeting of P.A.W. have descended into the dusts, and with them the aims and purposes of the Grand Scheme. Modern woman, or a segment thereof, alienated from the designs of her forebearers, aspires to what she now envisions as male vocational "prerogatives," and the Feminist Movement is undertaken.

The Grand Matriarchal Scheme is obvious whimsy, yet the theme of an actual Patriarchal Cabal, both explicit and implicit in much of Women's Liberation writing, presents only the other side of this fantastic coin. It betrays either a lack of knowledge, or a gross misunderstanding, of the realities of the individual male's existence, for Man's Wonderful Workaday World is sometimes less than the unremitting pleasure it is reputed to be.

The image of the Provider, a critical component of the Masculine Mystique, has been uncritically accepted by males as a fact of their glorified lives. The Dominance Drive, the Achiever Complex, and the Myth of Male Superiority find the Provider a superb instrument for their expression.

The Mystique has enabled the Provider with an ethic: The more productive and prolific his endeavors, the more virtuous the man. Hard work, ambition, and diligence are extolled as inherently "good," since they further the purpose of the Provider, while idleness, "unproductive" leisure, and a lack of financial success become somewhat sinful, tainted, and "bad." Under expressions of sorrow for the man "who worked himself to death" lie feelings of admiration for a fallen hero. That he may have been foolish, more neurotic than noble, is seldom thought or stated. He must have been "a good man."

The Darwinian era of economic thought has left its imprint of "the survival of the fittest," with the implication that those who "make it" are most fit, not only as economic venturers, but also as human beings. Consideration, friendliness, and charity, should they impede production, are deemed little more than naive notions indulged in by "failures" and fools. The Mystique has ordained performance and success as among the noblest of male virtues. How else can one explain the crushing work schedules and the devotion of most of a man's waking hours to the pursuit of vocational success? "Economic necessity," the usual reply, is insufficient. Too many men work, or would work if they could, over and beyond the time required to provide a reasonable standard of living. Furthermore, each step up the ladder makes necessities out of prior luxuries, and higher standards and greater luxuries loom beyond the horizon. Must one display the most expensive Scotch in his bar? Does a man require the costliest hi-fi set or the fastest camera? Wouldn't a less expensive model, purchased with less labor and time, serve as well? But the Provider must keep working and amassing, and his goals are unlimited. For the Provider, "life" and "work" are synonyms.

The Bhagavad Gita tells us: "What is work? and what is not work? are questions that perplex the wisest of men." The dictionary defines work as: "1) Physical or mental effort exerted to do or make something; purposeful activity; labor; toil." It is an obligatory activity, the essential purpose of which is to provide the essentials of life for a man and his family. While the fortunate male derives varying degrees of personal satisfaction from his labor, surveys indicate that 60 to 80 percent of workers are dissatisfied with their vocational lot, and would switch jobs if given the opportunity.

From St. Benedict's benediction: "To work is to pray," to Aldous Huxley's: "Like every man of sense and good feeling, I abominate work," work has been alternately lauded and lambasted. Euripides referred to toil as "the sire of fame," while William Faulkner wryly noted: "One of the saddest things is that the only thing a man can do for eight hours a day, day after day, is work. You can't eat for eight hours a day, nor drink for eight hours a day, nor make love for eight hours." Although most men find their labors to be somewhere between these extremes of Heaven and Hell, it would appear that more are aware of the heat of the Inferno than feel the flutter of angel's wings.

From the standpoint of St. Benedict, it might be said that a man's occupation gives him a sense of identity, akin to "Who are you?", "I'm a lawyer." It has a regulatory effect on one's life, allowing achievement and mastery in a specific area. Work encourages the man to develop his potentials and to derive satisfaction from the exercise of his talents. Moreover, work affords the obsessional personality a socially applauded outlet for a neurotic drive. In our civilization, the successful worker achieves self-esteem, a validation of his worth as a human being. There are, unfortunately, too few agencies in our society that lend themselves to this type of validation. A man satisfied with his job finds it one of his central interests, has a social relationship with his co-workers, and is motivated to seek satisfaction and gratification from his exertions. An interesting and secure job diminishes feelings of insecurity, helplessness, and inferiority. Like it or not, a boy is raised to feel that his selfworth is inextricably bound to his vocation and to his standing on the socioeconomic ladder, a derivative of his job. Of course, this can be pushed to extremes. Donald, a thirty-year-old dentist, was summering on Fire Island, a fairly sophisticated spa and retreat for the tired brains of Manhattan. Since his parents were intrigued by the Island's reputation, lurid and otherwise, he invited them out for the day. Close friends generously gave a cocktail party in their honor. On a spacious veranda, glasses clinked and martinis mixed with bullshots and screwdrivers. Praises of "Donald" were liberally directed toward his wide-eyed parents. During the occasional lull which marks the tempo at such affairs, his mother, her breast swelling with pride, meekly inquired: "Doesn't anyone call him 'Doctor'?" Donald prayed for a quick and merciful death, and proceeded to drown himself in vodka, wishing again and again that he had become a stockbroker. Apparently occupational status does have its limitations, and the wise man realizes them.

If we approach work from the viewpoint of a Faulkner or a Huxley, we confront alienation, boredom, and psychological slavery. In *The House of the Dead*, Dostoevsky agonized that: "To crush, to annihilate a man utterly, to inflict on him the most horrible of punishments so that the most ferocious murderer would shudder at it and dread it beforehand, one need only give him work of an absolutely, completely useless and irrational character." How many men have employment approximating this job description? The factory and the assembly line, the toll booths, the manned elevators, the bureaucratic non-work, and countless other employments, peopled by unnoticed and unremembered faces, crush the mind, annihilate the spirit, and impose the sentence of a vacuous existence on those employed in them. The consequence of this unhappy state is a sense of alienation, in which a man is divorced from his humanness, feeling more an inanimate "thing" than a human being. While some men, consciously "make a deal" with themselves to "put in their time," receive their paychecks, and finally their pensions, other men are aware only of a nagging dissatisfaction or depression, or know that something isn't quite right with their lives. Alienation, present in varying degrees, is the modern-day version of the working man's Hell.

The alienated Provider is a man holding charter memberships in the Thank God It's Friday Society and the

Sunday Night Blues Anonymous. Friday afternoon is Liberation Day, while Sunday evening induces a heavy lump in his chest. His weekdays are perceived as a tour of duty on a prison ship, shuttling from Lassitude to Boredom and back. He finds his job monotonous, and his attention seesaws from the work at hand to fantasies of better things and happier times. He frequently forgets what he is doing, for his activity has minimal interest to him. Since only a few men are involved in decision-making processes, the Provider has a pervasive sense of powerlessness, which is manifested as a feeling of being too closely supervised and a resentment that he has little or no opportunity to effectuate meaningful changes in the work process. When extra effort on his part is neither recognized nor rewarded, his petulance rises, with increased absenteeism, industrial sabotage, and occupational depressions as the consequences. This woeful state of affairs is epitomized by the assembly line, in which the work performed is meticulously dictated by the nature and the construction of the line. The worker has no control over the tempo of his work, and any deviation is intrinsically disruptive. Further dissatisfaction with one's employment is evidenced by a feeling of marking time before making that move to a better job (which seldom takes place), alternating with a feeling that the job is a dead end. Although the worker requires validation of his human worth, his vocational pursuit is perceived to be meaningless. He finds little significance in his contribution to the final product, and avoids discussing his job with friends, assuming that they too would find it dull. The task itself may make little sense to him; an elevator operator presses a button with no greater skill than his passenger.

Most men seek some degree of personal creativity, growth, and expression from the activities in which they engage. To the extent that these opportunities are absent in their employment, a sense of estrangement is created. The knowledge that one can be replaced by a machine, or easily substituted for, adds little to a man's spirit or dignity. If he feels of little worth, he acts accordingly, and slipshod work is the consequence. Not feeling responsible for the production of a quality product, his sense of "who cares" eventuates in the Monday-produced automotive lemon or the unplayable television set. Of the several "assemble-it-yourself" items which I have lately and lamentedly purchased, the majority were either defectively produced or were packaged with vital parts missing. Why? Who cared?

The psychological enslavement of the Provider to his occupation is more pervasive than is commonly realized, and is best exemplified by the Retirement Depression. There was a time when Stanley had been a handsome, gregarious, and dynamic editor-in-chief of a leading magazine. Having climbed his way from newspaper copy boy to become a leading figure in publishing circles, he had straddled the summit. Under his sixteen-hour-per-day aegis, the publication's circulation had flourished and its quality had appreciated. Totally immersed in his industry, the idea of eventual retirement was passingly dealt with by flip references to "bridge and golf." Inevitably, retirement day arrived, and shockingly so. The testimonials over, he soon found that golf had been interesting only when business had been discussed on the back nine, and that bridge could become a deadly bore when played day after day. As time went on, it became increasingly oppressive. The precipitating fuse, that final fillip which ushers in a full-blown depression, was the first issue of the publication with Stanley's name missing from the masthead. His distraught wife and children described him as "a changed man overnight." The dynamo had had his plug pulled out.

During our initial meeting, he alternately paced, writhed, and sat, his face drawn and expressionless. A previously normal blood pressure had soared some sixty millimeters, and sleep had become a dim memory. His appetite had disappeared, along with any sexual interest. "The only thing I can tell you is that my name on that masthead always seemed like my sheriff's badge; and without the badge I felt like nothing. And I can't accept the idea of being a nothing." The symbol of the badge was striking. He had been a rather puny and studious youth, not particularly successful with his peers, and had developed a compensatory fantasy life in which he was admired and commanded respect. The lawman motif was present in this childhood daydream. In addition to its power connotation, it was an exemplary derivative of a strongly developed conscience. Stanley had always set high standards for himself and for others, and these standards controlled his life. Inability to meet them had always been poorly tolerated. His place on the masthead had signified the admiration, authority, and control which were so dearly prized. Divested of his sheriff's badge, he saw himself as "a powerless eunuch." Heroes who lose their laurel wreaths understandably become depressed.

Stanley typifies the man who utilizes his job to establish an identity and to keep this identity vital and alive. As part of the contract, however, he becomes enslaved to his position. When the job terminates, his identity evaporates, and he becomes the good plow-horse who is lost without his plow. Even the sympathy and understanding proffered by his listener are of no avail. When a life has no meaning, solicitude and concern mean little. The man who stakes his life on his Provider role takes a greater gamble than he realizes, and the piper must eventually be paid.

The Mystique loudly proclaims the male as the lord and master of his economic domain. The popular myth has him doling out the pesos with a palsied and parsimonious palm, with his wife bravely making ends meet on this sufferance. But is this verity or merely propaganda? While the Provider labors in the fields "by the sweat of his brow," and ravages the earth for his family's sustenance, it is his wife who dispenses 85 percent of the family income. Not the Provider, but his female kin own 65 percent of all the nation's savings accounts, 74 percent of titles to suburban homes, and 65 percent of the nation's private wealth.

A prime complaint voiced by many women is that their husbands have no idea of the cost of the various items in the family budget. The complaint is valid, and has been the cause of innumerable family squabbles. Unfortunately, the Provider has become estranged from the utilization of the very money he has earned. On those rare days when a husband accompanies his wife on a shopping tour, the store manager waxes ecstatic. The bill is invariably higher, with the husband happily engaging in impulse buying and in the purchase of the more expensive items, despite the fact that their cost astonishes him. It is as though he is celebrating the expenditure of his earnings like a vacationer for whom money has lost its meaning.

An ultimate measure of the Provider is his paycheck. "Figures don't lie," as the saying goes, and the numbers on a check become a mathematical calibration of the Provider's prowess, akin to the number of pounds a weight lifter can press. In 1971, the median family income of the American family was $10,285. However, $10,971 was

deemed the necessary minimum for an intermediate standard of living. Furthermore, consider the minimal $80,000
to $150,000 or more needed to raise two children from
birth through college, a figure compiled by the Commis-
sion on Population Growth and the American Future.
From these figures, can we infer that most men are failures in their appointed task? What pall does it cast over
their psyches? To make the impossible even worse, we
are living in an era of rapidly rising expectations, in which
accepted and expected standards of living outsoar the
capacities of the wage earner. Those in the younger age
range are consequently too often heavily in debt, with
many falling increasingly behind in the struggle to get
even. In epidemic fashion, anticipation erodes the discipline of reason. The theme of "I am entitled to" sweeps
over the muted "I have earned," and indebtedness becomes a way of life. Accountants and tax lawyers note
that even men in the $50,000 to $75,000 wage bracket
are chronically in debt, and seldom have any substantial
savings. *New York* magazine once ran a lead article on
how to go broke on $80,000 per year. Surrounded by
images of affluence (how many small kitchens or living
rooms are portrayed on television or movie screens?),
men feel compelled to procure and display them or suffer
a loss of prestige. The syndrome of the large house, expensive clothing, and an empty refrigerator is a pathetic expression of a topsy-turvy value structure. In the halcyon
days of my internship, ambulance calls sped me to many
slum dwellings, dingy and barely furnished, inhabited by
undernourished children. It was not a rarity for family
members to follow the ambulance back to the hospital in
expensive and exquisitely polished automobiles. The
appurtenances had taken priority over the appetite.

The wedding of the male with the Provider image
was detailed by Dr. Juanita Kreps, a professor of econom-

ics at Duke University, in a lecture to the American Psychiatric Association entitled "Modern Man and His Instinct for Workmanship." Dr. Kreps's thesis was that while modern technology has diminished work time, the higher earners work longer hours. These "long-houred workers," professionals and executives, are pressured to forego vacations and to increase the time and effort devoted to work. Blue-collar workers evidence a preference for more paid work rather than leisure time, and keenly compete for overtime. One-third of high-income Providers work fifty-five or more hours per week, and business executives average fifty hours, excluding entertaining and travel time. She suggested that the work imperative may have become "an unbalancing influence in the lives of the long-hours men," and that they have become "too concerned with work, too little committed to play, and too scornful of the gay and lighthearted." It is also to be noted that men under forty-five who are subject to deadlines, marked competition, and long working hours have higher levels of cholesterol in their blood and a higher occurrence of heart attacks than do their fellows in less stressful vocational milieus, and that this stress may be facilitated by intense ambition itself.

During his sojourn in the occupational jungle, the Provider is beset by numerous pitfalls and snares which entrap his psyche into one disability after the other.

A man's attitude toward his position is determined by his individual personality interwoven with the aspects of the job itself. Security, advancement, working conditions, wages, and benefits are immediate and evident considerations. The quality of supervision, the opportunity to participate in the channels of communication with the higher echelons, the intrinsic elements of the job (travel, entertaining, etc.), and the opportunity to identify oneself as part of an organization are less obvious, but are, perhaps, of equal importance. While in Japan, I had the opportunity to visit factories and other places of business. Small Shinto and Buddhist shrines were inconspicuously placed within the factory complexes. "Why are there shrines in industrial or commercial locations?" I asked my guide. Somewhat taken aback by the naiveté of my question, he simply answered: "For the employees to pray for the success of the company, of course." The paternalism of Japanese firms, combined with their liberal bonuses, increase the worker's identification with his firm and play a major role in the industrial success of postwar Japan.

To the extent that the above necessities are unmet, the Provider will ache. The older worker worries about job security, eschews change, and fears competition. The middle-ager is concerned with his status, and must come to grips with the fact that his economic peak has probably been reached; while the younger employee is preoccupied with advancement opportunity and the possibility of effectuating change. Apparently it is difficult to satisfy everyone. The most frequently voiced concerns of polled employees were failure to advance, how they would exist when they were too old to work, temporary layoffs, the loss of their jobs, and the lack of skills required to perform their work. Thus, upward mobility and security were perceived as major concerns for the Provider.

In the happy event that the worker is promoted to supervisor or foreman, his family will rejoice over their enhanced status and the higher figure on his paycheck. The Provider, however, is faced with new dilemmas. Paid by management to oversee his former peers, he finds himself in a role conflict. Where do his loyalties now lie: with the company which pays his salary or with his former fellows? Let us suppose that he successfully balances these conflicting loyalties and advances further to the executive level. He has now achieved high status and financial reward, but one noteworthy failure in judgment can undo years of hard work. The resultant pressures are apt to produce a paralysis in decision-making, chronic anxiety, and an uneasy relationship with those upon whom he must rely. A survey of executive tensions by the Life Extension Institute of New York in 1971 showed increased insecurity, dissatisfaction with job progress, more worry about job decisions, and a greater alcoholic intake than were found in a similar survey in 1958.

At this level, the injection of ethical strains adds additional stress. Should a man lie when taking a series of psychological tests for a preferred position? Should the applicant admit to preferring *Playboy* or *Sports Illustrated* when he knows the company is looking for the reader of *Fortune* and *Reader's Digest*? If prostitutes are regularly procured by his competitors, ought he to follow suit and strain his marriage and his morals, or should he demur and risk both the loss of his job and the impoverishment of his family? If industrial espionage is thrust upon him, should he "go along" or inform the police? If his company blithely continues to produce a potentially dangerous product, what course should a man follow? Are his business dealings to reflect his personal morality, or should they approximate the ethics of a poker game? The answers only appear easy; living through the situation is an entirely different matter.

While the aforementioned considerations are built into the occupational structure, the personality of the individual Provider is infused into the vocational blender, adding to the rise of psychic disabilities. One business magazine reports that character traits were accountable for 90 percent of the causes of firings and 76 percent of the rationale behind refused promotions by one major company. The Provider's personality makeup is involved in numerous occupational syndromes and neuroses. Emotional illness is felt to cause 25 to 35 percent of work absences. Alcoholism is found in well over two million workers, with an average of four to five missed weeks of work per year per alcoholic employee. Impulsive character traits account for a large share of accidents. "Low back syndromes" and compensation neuroses are often associated with depressions and feelings of persecution. Supervisors become anxious, depressed, and tend to develop psychosomatic complaints due to responsibility and role conflicts. Paranoid traits among workers' representatives may produce morale problems and unnecessary work stoppages.

In the more creatively-oriented occupations, the Provider faces the problem of work inhibition, in which, regardless of the heroism of his endeavors, his creative productivity is stifled. These inhibitions are perhaps even more commonly seen in psychiatric practice than are the sexual inhibitions. One of the better known work inhibitions is "writer's block." A heretofore successful playwright was unable to complete the last act of a play scheduled for rehearsal in the immediate future. On approaching the typewriter, his mind simply went blank, for no ostensible reason. On investigation, it was soon obvious that his hostility toward his ex-wife was even more devastating than he had realized, and, unfortunately, his ex-spouse would reap a financial windfall if the play proved to be a hit. While chopping firewood at a vacation cabin, a friend advised him to envision his ex-wife's head atop each cord of wood. His energies waxed vigorous and fierce, and he enjoyed every blessed moment of it. The last act was promptly completed, and the rapidly completed masterpiece ran a full season on Broadway.

Work inhibitions are the symptoms of unconscious or

dimly perceived anxieties. Fears of success, failure, or competition conjure up painful consequences, which are averted by work paralysis. The thought of "failure" is particularly abhorrent to those whose sense of self-esteem is particularly fragile, as if a single missed effort would confirm the underlying abysmal image they have of themselves. Ergo, best not to make the attempt. Ancient childhood rivalries with brothers or sisters are played out in the workaday world, and their adult remnants may be so unacceptable that winning in the vocational scramble may be threatening. A major advertising firm had a vice-presidency up for grabs. A talented copywriter suddenly became incapable of producing his usual incandescent idea, and lost his chance for the promotion. He was an older brother who had been reared with the parental imperative to take care of his younger sibling, and never, under any circumstances, to compete with him. His competitors for the job were all younger males. When a man has feared his father or other older and more powerful figures in his life, "success" may symbolize a forbidden conquest of these potent figures and may consequently be abjured. Following a promotion over the heads of more senior members of an industrial firm, a man developed recurrent nightmares in which he was destroyed by ocean waves rushing over his head and by a variety of other catastrophic events.

In a yesterday that seems a million years ago, the Provider reaped more than monetary compensation from his labors. He could take pride in the products of his craftmanship, and paternally pass the lore inherited from his father on to his offspring. His business was within a reasonable distance of his home, so that his activities were seen, understood, and appreciated by his kin and kith. The modern-day Provider, on the other hand, is employed in vocations which are often beyond the ken of his family. Try explaining computer programming, the deft social dance of the account executive, or the complexities of the plastics laboratory to a young son. Furthermore, the Provider has become a phantasmal transient who arrives home after long hours on some commuter conveyance, haggard and wanting only peace and quiet, hardly fit for even conversation with a spouse and children hungry for interaction with him. But the treadmill keeps running, and the Provider must keep apace.

Somewhere in this favored and affluent land there are men who look forward to Monday mornings and who derive satisfaction and stimulation from their occupational endeavors, but there are many more who don't. Many of these denizens of the "world of the ulcer and the coronary" find it difficult or "unmanly" to admit to their dissatisfactions, anxieties, and stresses, for the Provider image is deemed intrinsic to their masculinity. As a consequence, their sufferings are accentuated and remedial action is inhibited. The Provider's woeful workhorse theme has been too passively accepted by generations of men. Responsibility, in its deepest sense, is met by a man adapting his vocation to his life, and not vice versa. The effort to achieve this balance would set the Provider on the path to becoming a truly liberated man.

# 4

# The Sex Life of a Penis

*The Disenfranchised Phallus*

THE SEXUAL CHRONICLE of the twentieth century is no longer simply an account of how often how many vaginas play hostess to how many penises. The crux of the revolution it reports is the increasing respect accorded to the female sexual drive and the consequent backlash directed at male sexuality generally and the penis especially. The sweeping change from the antediluvian notion that "ladies lie still" to the contemporary feminist frenzy for more bumptious orgasms is as emancipatory in scope as was the Magna Carta. It has certainly touched more people than did that princely concession. College dormitories now invite coeducational cohabitation, virginity has become a questionable virtue, and varied versions of a feminine Declaration of Independence have become enshrined in a deluge of books, periodicals, films, and the like. All that remains is the denouement, its gradual integration into our cultural thought and institutions. The exhilaration and the ecstasy of the bold challenge eases into pedestrian practicality.

Every upheaval, like every election, has its winners and its losers, the victors and the casualties. The sexual rights, and perhaps even the erotic supremacy, of women are presently in the ascendancy, and the clitoris will never again be regarded as a second-class phallus. The orgastic potential of women is now scientifically proclaimed as unquestionably more profound than the male's. Caricatured as a piddling appendage attached to a chauvinist male, the horn of the unicorn has finally acquiesced to the lotus blossom.

But every successful revolt creates its dispossessed. Adam after Eden, Napoleon at Elba, Thomas Dewey after Harry Truman: what is the lot of the disinherited? The phallus appears as a principal casualty of our most recent social upheaval. Stranded by the Mystique's phallocentric propaganda, his heroic pretensions reduced to human proportions, the phallus has become a fallen champion. The disenfranchised penis emerges as the prototypic antihero who must deny in order to survive.

Under the aegis of the Mystique, the penis was placed on a superhuman pedestal, deified and adulated throughout the centuries. The Hindu god Siva was proclaimed the possessor of a phallus of infinite size by Vishnu and Brahma. I would presume that this was the trendsetter. Oriental art traditionally portrayed the phallus as having dimensions equivalent to man's other extremities. The Greeks referred to the male sexual organ as *aidoion*, the inspirer of holy awe, while the Romans used its representations to decorate their homes and constructed mighty stone phalluses to delineate land boundaries. Early Church fathers celebrated the fertile phallus by ornamenting church property with its replicas, while some African tribes collected the phalluses of their foes rather than their heads.

While this attention and flattery had its seductive aspects, it contained the germ of the eventual fall of the penis. How, after all, does one live up to the infinite?

Being human is difficult enough: assuming a godlike posture brings down deific wrath. Hubris, that aroma of
arrogance exuding from excessive pride, was the downfall
of many a figure in mythology. It has also resulted in the
chronic downwardness of a number of disillusioned
penises.

One of the more trenchant observations of the erotic
was W. C. Fields's: "There may be some things better than
sex, and some things may be worse, but there is nothing
exactly like it." In truth, it is a unique experience. While
other biologic drives, hunger, thirst, and elimination, are
life-sustaining, have immediacy attached to them, and are
essentially solitary enterprises, man's sexual impulse can
be indefinitely postponed or even entirely eschewed, and
is generally performed in concert with another human
being. The consequent plasticity of the slowly evolving
sexual drive allows a culture to more deeply permeate it
and to mold it in accordance with whatever social relationships the culture has opted for. The aim of man's sexuality is a pleasant activity, his society determines the
ground rules of the game.

The two principal varieties of erotic experience are
recreational sex and relational sex. The sex life of the
penis reflects this duality, consisting of a nucleus of the
recreational, surrounded by a host of relational elements
which can either expand or devour it. A venerable psychiatric adage advises that a man has two heads, and when
he uses both at the same time, he's in for trouble. The
head between the legs is the recreational seat, while the
head between the ears houses the relational. A well-made
sexual cocktail is a fusion of these two elements, consisting of a recreational base, to which a jigger or two of the
relational has been added, depending on one's taste. Too
much of the additive indicates a poorly mixed and stifling
concoction which a gentleman should return to the bar-

tender. It has been the unhappy fate of the contemporary male and his well-intentioned phallus that his sexual center has been insidiously forced upward from the crotch toward the brain.

Recreational sex is experienced as enjoyable play, happily hedonistic, and emphasizes the sensate response of the participants. A phallic frolic, it is of no cosmic import, and free of compulsivity, imperatives, and guilt. It can be identified by adjectives such as "lusty," "earthy," "lecherous," "sensual," "voluptuous," and dozens of other intriguing terms which have unfortunately acquired a pejorative connotation in a togetherness-centered culture which is committed to the containment of recreational sex.

Society's vendetta against pornography is a case in point. Pornography is usually defined as material designed to appeal to the prurient interest, to produce erotic arousal while devoid of any redeeming social value. Apparently society cannot tolerate specifically sexual play, naked, uncamouflaged, and divorced from any social commitment or relational obligations. Yet pornography is far more beneficial to the individual and his society than it is conceivably harmful. For those pornophiles who enjoy literary or cinematic titillation, it supplies an enjoyable though innocent sensual excitation, which normally pales if overdone. Men and women viewing films of repeated sexual intercourse quickly become bored. When Denmark legalized pornography in 1969, a boom was anticipated at the bookstalls; but the boom proved to be a bust, sales fell off, and the prime customers became the tourists rather than the citizens. Apparently pornography is a self-limited experience which exerts no forest-fire effect on the passions. Sexual criminals, the rapists and pedophiles (child molesters), not only have had less exposure to erotic material than the rest of the population, but they are also less reactive to it. Indeed, Denmark showed a significant drop in sexual crimes in the years following 1969. Exposure to erotic material during adolescence probably diminishes criminality rather than encourages it.

From the standpoint of the pornophile, pornography provides a multitude of blessings. It supplies diversion and pleasure; it acts as a transient sexual stimulant, more effectively than alcohol or marihuana; it serves an educational function, bridging the gaps which parents and schools find difficult to fill; it encourages variety and experimentation, usually a welcome addition to stultified sexual lives; and provides a masturbatory outlet to those who might destructively act out their antisocial sexual impulses. Pornophiles, as a group, are usually sensitive people with a capacity for fantasy, both estimable traits.

One legitimate objection to pornography concerns children. Flooding a child with more sexuality than he can absorb, understand, and handle might conceivably upset the gradual process of sexual maturation. Why not, then, simply make pornography less readily accessible, but establish it as a legitimate commodity to be obtained by those of requisite age, under other than the sleazy conditions which now surround supply sources?

Society's adjudication of pornography as "hard-core" only exemplifies its hard-core resistance to the concept of sex as play. The popular pornographic film *Deep Throat* was banned as obscene in Manhattan Criminal Court. In his condemnation, the judge noted that it "was as explicit and as exquisite as life." Bizarre! This medieval obsession with the subservience of the passionate to the parochial provides one more obstacle which the penis must traverse in its battle for functional survival.

Relational sex, moving from the sensate to the cerebrate, places the emphasis primarily upon the "meaning" of a sexual activity as it relates to another person, institution, or thing. The relational factor adds a grab-bag element to man's sexual responses. A cooperating brain may provide a positive reinforcement to the penis, with the addition of affection, fantasy, and the active engagement with one's partner in an exploratory adventure designed to increase the genital response. But brains aren't necessarily cooperative. They contain the debris of early childhood misunderstandings and mishandlings; they have been exposed to the machinations of the Mystique and other forms of antisexual cultural conditioning; they are often stuffed with imperatives, the "shouldn'ts," the "ought-tos," the guilts, and the assorted hang-ups which have been the lot of "civilized" man for centuries. Brains deal not only with the penis, but also with dimly understood archetypal parents, the injunctions of the Church and the law. When cerebral compromises are effectuated between these protagonists, it is frequently the penis which pays the price. The brain may be a noble organ, but it is sexually unreliable.

Recreational sex ruled the roost until a few centuries ago. In the good old days, open sexuality was fairly commonplace, allowing for a generous genital fulfillment for both men and women. Public nudity, nonvirginity, pre- and extramarital erotic dalliance were assumed, since sex was regarded as just another bodily appetite, like eating and drinking, and was unencumbered with life-long emotional and legal commitments. The ancient Hebrews, primarily concerned with family and parenthood, placed no proscriptions against premarital sex in the Old Testament, and barely tolerated perpetual virginity in the Talmud. The Egyptians countenanced incest, expected women to partake in the initiation of amorous activities, and not only decorated their temples with explicitly sexual motifs, but supplied their dead with pornography and dildos to amuse themselves with as well. Sparta encouraged nude public dancing between youths of both sexes, and the ensuing sexual freedom was not unexpected. Nor was Athens noted for its sexual restraint. Religious festivals were associated with socially sanctioned promiscuity, and the hetairai, the acme of Greek courtesanship, enjoyed a higher social standing than most Greek matrons. At the height of the Roman Empire, with marriage distinctly regarded as a political and economic institution, sexual activity continued to be more recreational and less institutional. This general state of affairs continued through the Dark Ages, until the twelfth century gave rise to the Medieval Church and the ideal of courtly or romantic love.

From its inception, the Christian Church conducted a crusade against the flesh and the Devil by extolling celibacy, virginity, and self-denial. Christ lauded "those which have made themselves eunuchs for the kingdom of heaven's sake." Even marital relations were accepted only with great reluctance. In the Epistle to the Corinthians, St. Paul advises: "It is good for a man not to touch a woman. Nevertheless, to avoid fornication, let every man have his own wife, and let every woman have her own husband. . . . I say therefore to the unmarried and widows, it is good for them if they abide even as I. But if they cannot contain, let them marry; for it is better to marry than to burn." The Church fathers believed that the passions of this world distracted men from the Paradise of the next, and that the suppression of the bodily was the strongest inducement to the devotion to the heavenly. As the Church's intrusion into the bedroom progressed, increasing injunctions were leveled against full sexual expression, with imperatives toward self-control pushed further and further. "The" position to be used in coitus and the hours of the day in which this might take place were prescribed. When the Medieval Church developed in power and prestige, matters grew so gruesome that marital relations were illegal for 203 days per year. Sundays, Wednesdays, and Fridays, plus forty days before Easter and forty days prior to Christmas, were declared sexless by some divine fiat. During this period of acute sexual repression, flagellation, hysteria, witchcraft, stigmatae, and other socially sanctioned forms of madness replaced calmer sexual sporting.

The ideal of courtly or romantic love grew with the development of the Medieval Church. Men were encouraged to adore an ideal, untouchable woman rather than to romp with a real one. Many commentators attribute the birth of the romantic ideal to the emerging veneration of Mary. When in 1937 Havelock Ellis wrote: "The sexual embrace can only be compared with music and with prayer," he was merely giving voice to a twentieth-century version of the sanctification of the relational element in the sexual process initiated during the Middle Ages.

The penis continued to prevail under obviously adverse circumstances. Despite his physical limitations, regardless of conflicting messages from testes, cerebrum, and God, he gave a visceral performance. For once, the Mystique had come to man's assistance. Labeling him an olympian Sexual Athlete who performed feats of wonder and awe, the Mystique concocted a penile placebo, a sugar-coated illusion calculated to provide a harassed athlete with that second wind enabling him to exert extra effort to convert the expectable performance into the unforgettable moment. But the life span of any placebo is limited, and the past decade has seen the Mystique, for once, mystified.

With the weight of current comparison of male and female sexual capacities veering toward the female, and with feminist writers demeaning the masculine with such unkindly cuts as: "Nature seems to him to have practised a niggardly economy when she came to designing man, in contrast to the munificence she lavished on the making of woman," the penis has struggled valiantly to retain his integrity and self-esteem. It is little wonder that more than a few have retired from the fray, *hors de combat.*

The current sexual tide has produced swells of sexual talk and has resulted in more women becoming more insistent on deriving more sexual gratification. In fact, the crescendo is mounting to such a pitch that the quest for the orgiastic orgasm, or even multiple orgasms, no longer suffices. Germaine Greer, for example, exhorts women to "hold out not just for orgasm, but for ecstasy." If only she defined her term. The obsessional component inherent in these endeavors is projected onto the penis as an increased demand for greater production from women who have already been informed that their capacities are all but limitless. Unfortunately, these exhortations neatly blend into the penile illusions fostered by the Mystique.

The contemporary penis finds himself the focal point of converging imperatives. The feminist call for infinite erotic fulfillment collides with his finite physical capacities; echos of the Mystique's evocation of the Sexual Athlete abut against inclinations toward being human; and testicular urges for the recreational contrast with the brain's emphasis on the relational. Few, if any, organs function well in a conflictual environment, and the penis is no exception. A clarifying question might then be: "What can a man reasonably ask of his penis, and vice versa?"

## The Average Expectable Penis

The penis is a rather remarkable instrument that houses three functions, procreation, recreation, and urination, in one small but expansive container. Women are more generously endowed with several organs to perform the same functions. Their vagina and uterus procreate, the urethra urinates, and the clitoris is there just for fun.

From the anatomical and physiological standpoints, we probably understand more about the functioning of the phallus than we do about any other organ in the body. Its central canal, the urethra, is partly surrounded by spongy cavernous tissue which simply engorges with blood during sexual arousal, enlarging the penis from its average four-inch length to an erectile size of approximately six inches. The increase in arterial blood supply which accomplishes this feat is primarily mediated by nerves emerging from the sacral (lower) segment of the spinal cord, responding either to reflex stimulation from nerve endings in the penis or to cerebral excitation which travels down the length of the spinal cord to activate these sacral neurons. A randy dream or erotic reverie could arouse the appropriate center in the brain to send its message down through the cord and inspire the sacral nerves. The early stage of excitation results in erection, some elevation of the testicles, and a flushing of the chest and neck. As excitation increases, a plateau stage is reached, during which the testes enlarge some 50 percent, and a feeling of orgasmic inevitability is experienced. Finally orgasm occurs, during which everything at first seems to expand and then contract. The glands (prostate and seminal vesicles), the sphincter muscles (urethral and anal), the urethra, and the penis all spastically contract, ejaculation occurs, and the penis subsequently eases into the resolution phase, in which all the elements revert to their normal conditions and proportions. The penis becomes refractory to further excitation for varying periods of time, depending on one's age, physical condition, and degree of satiation.

It is the good fortune of women, who have their own version of each of these stages, that they possess a negligible refractory period. They are able to effortlessly shuttle from orgasm to plateau, and back to orgasm until a state of physical exhaustion is reached. While the average male is spent after one, or a splendid second orgasm, per sexual congress, a woman may have as many as six or sixty orgasms should she be so inclined and enjoy the physical stamina. This has been somewhat disconcerting even to those penises that are able to maintain their erectile state for many moments beyond the usual two to five minutes which the ordinary male member remains within the vaginal vault before that final spasm. Once again, the good performance cannot compete with the infinite, and intimations of inadequacy seep into the sensitivities of even the most prolific of phalluses. The physiological fact of relative orgastic limitations has become the Waterloo of stoutly held pretensions of penile supremacy. To give the penis his due, however, it must be recognized that male and female sexual responses are no more comparable than an aged Scotch and a fine wine. Male sexuality is characterized by a greater immediacy and urgency, while the female is more involved with a gradual summation and extended capacity. Both satisfy, but each in its unique way.

Although the male ego has been coerced by the compulsion to acquire plaudits for facility between the bedsheets and lives in horror of inadequacy or aberration, there simply are no valid criteria for the "normal" or "average" penile performance. Changing times and customs, and alterations in desires and demands throughout one's life span, make such judgments impossible. Statistics may tell us the average penile size, but there are normal variations which have little to do with adequacy of function, since the vagina obligingly expands to nestle about whatever dimensions its entrant possesses. Since the vast majority of a woman's sexually responsive nerve endings are concentrated at her periphery (the clitoris, the outer area of the vagina and its surrounding tissues), depth of penetration is rather academic. Kinsey found that 77 percent of men were sexually aroused by observing pictures of sexual activity. Are the other 23 percent therefore "abnormal"? To respond affirmatively would only confuse "average" with "normalcy."

Similarly, the current statistical approach has the unfortunate side effect of emphasizing quantity (how frequent and how long) over quality (how satisfying). It is of immense research value, however, and some results are highly provocative. For example, the male in his twenties averages 2.6 sexual experiences (intercourse, masturbation, petting, etc.) per week. Let's assume that he confines these to intercourse, and is a reasonably facile performer, with each experience lasting approximately twenty minutes from foreplay to finale. He spends more time per week watching *Bonanza* on television than in achieving bonanzas in bed. By the time he reaches his forties, this statistic is reduced to 1.5 weekly coital connections. He spends more time shaving than he does copulating. Lest this appear too selected a sampling, one which excludes the rutted randiness of hot-blooded youth, let's invite the college crowd to join in. The 1971 Playboy College Poll of three thousand students in sixty colleges revealed that 50 percent of males and 60 percent of females have either no intercourse or less than one experience per month. Only 16 percent of males and 15 percent of females had intercourse on an eight times or more monthly frequency. Yet the vast majority of those who experienced sexual relations found their most recent sexual experience either satisfying or more satisfying than frustrating. To make matters even more interesting, while the poll found 5 percent fewer female virgins on campus than in the previous year, there were 5 percent more male virgins. Twenty-three percent of the male respondents had never had intercourse, while 44 percent of the women had held on to their virginity. Truly an academic orgy!

Let these few figures sink in for a moment; mentally digest them. Has the American male become repressed and desexualized? Or is sex just one of many biologic activities that has its limited appetite. Have our cultural distortions created a sexual never-never land in which man's penile expectations are inveigled to extend far beyond his biologic propensities? Or are both true?

Apparently most penises are disinclined to quantitative heroics, but the question of reasonable expectations still remains. Perhaps a consensus would agree to the following: The adequate penis is capable of erection, and will enlarge given sufficient stimulation. It welcomes the company of women, and shrinks neither from them nor from the prospect of sexual intercourse. It has the requisite flexibility to exert enough control to adapt to most of the brain's exigencies so that the enjoyable moments can be reasonably lengthened. It functions better in a warm and affectionate milieu than in a detached, hostile, or punitive one. It operates, preferentially, spontaneously rather than being driven by obsessive ideas or compulsive rituals. Finally, the penis that fits these criteria will be regarded as a friendly organ of pleasure rather than an intransigent foe by its possessor. Should a man's sexual functioning fall within this happy framework, any addenda are just so much icing on the proverbial cake, be the frosting variations of oral-genital divertissement, a festive orgiastic fantasy, masturbation, or copulating while standing on one's head. Variety not only spices up one's life, it acts as a penile tonic as well.

## The Penis Under Siege

Contrary to the proclamations of the Mystique, male sexuality is a fragile entity, easily disrupted by childhood psychic mishandling and readily turned off by slight misadventures, a word, a gesture, or a hint of fatigue. From the functional standpoint, the penis is probably man's most vulnerable organ. Impotency, fetishism, transvestism, exhibitionism, and pedophilia are all but exclusively male phenomena. Homosexuality is thought to be at least twice as common in men as in women, and a premature orgasm, the *bête noire* of so many men, is nonexistent in women. The average penis partakes in some ten thousand orgasms during its lifetime. The remarkable thing is that so many function so well.

The brain has been increasingly referred to as man's true sexual organ since it has the capability of exercising an absolute veto power over penile activity. With this Damoclean sword constantly hanging over its head, with unconscious fears and inhibitions as ever-present potential explosive charges, it is understandable that the penis may view itself as under a chronic state of siege.

A rather dramatic demonstration of the besieged penis took place in Singapore, during the epidemic outbreak of Koro in the 1960s.

The male afflicted with Koro is gripped by the conviction that his penis is shrinking back into his abdomen, an unfortunate circumstance which will deprive him not only of his manhood but of his life as well, since death is assumed to coincide with this occurrence. This belief is shared by family and friends, who frantically seek medical attention for the afflicted penis. The spectacle of frenzied and desperate men, their penises grasped in their fists or fixed with ribbons tied tightly around their legs, or fastened to boxes or weights, is horrendous to contemplate. During this particular outbreak, the populace somehow implicated pork as a causative agent, and pork dealers consequently shut down and silently stole out of town for fear of reprisal.

Medical opinion considers Koro as a state of acute anxiety, precipitated by culturally determined fears of sexual overindulgence, which is generally, but not necessarily, limited to Southeast Asia, the Chinese province of Canton, and the Malay archipelago. The Koro syndrome provides an excellent example of the smooth cooperation among cultural, familial, and individual psychopathology to place the penis literally under siege. Incidentally, there was not one recorded case of any penis becoming lost in the dark recesses of anyone's abdomen. Most men recovered with appropriate psychiatric treatment, although many retained traces of their former anxiety. Western culture has had its manifestations of Koro, though its onslaught against the penis is less literal and therefore less appreciated.

Men handle stress by adopting one of four basic techniques. Ideally, they utilize their rationality and modify or adapt to the provocative situation. Should this approach be unattainable, they either assume the offense, take flight, or attempt to circumvent the problem. Their penises function in a similar fashion.

Given the existence of a sexual problem, the knowledge and understanding of it often allows for a reasonable and satisfactory solution. Adjustments can be made for misconceptions, irrational guilt feelings, and other oppressions. Should reason fail, the penis may be compelled to utilize one or several of the unconsciously motivated remaining alternatives.

It can preempt or attack—premature ejaculation ("Wham, bam, thank you, ma'am")—hit, run, and out; and quickly retire from the fray.

It can withdraw—into apathy or impotency, utilizing the bedroom as a four-walled arena to act out nonsexual needs such as dependency or power drives.

Finally, it can attempt to circumvent the conflict by changing its goal or direction, fixing instead on a deviation such as exhibitionism, fetishism, sado-masochism, or perhaps adopt a homosexual stance.

The last three options often place a man at odds with his sexuality, as if he were divided above and below the navel, with the two halves at war with each other.

The preemptive approach may produce such opposite extremes as Don Juanism and premature ejaculation. As a soldier may take heroic action to disprove his cowardice and fears, so may the sexually insecure male become a Don Juan to disprove inadequacy. The process is compulsive and never-ending; the next woman can always attest to the accuracy of his fear. Since the goal of his endeavors is unprovable, male-female interrelatedness becomes inconsequential and remains so as long as he pursues his quest.

Premature ejaculation, the most frequent of male sexual complaints, is more immediately disturbing and more poignantly experienced. Premature ejaculation is that unhappy condition in which the penis climaxes before the brain has given its assent. It is sometimes misdiagnosed by the male since unless ejaculation occurs at the moment of insertion or within three or four thrusts, the "prematurity" is dependent on the alacrity of his partner's satiatory capacities. More than a few men have deemed themselves premature after thirty to sixty minutes of penile thrusting into their partner's unresponsive vaginas. A sorry state indeed. The penis performed, but the brain was unappreciative. Given a more reactive female, the questioning of their adequacy would not arise. But the present-day responsibility of the male to satisfy places the onus upon him, and perspective fades.

Some men have sought solace in Kinsey's thesis, which regards rapid ejaculation as a "superior" response, equating any rapid action in living organisms as ipso facto evidence of a desirable property. If this superiority thesis is valid, why do not women share in this blessing, or are we still dealing with the issue of feminine inferiority? Furthermore, why should masturbation be less quicksilver than coitus? Let us eschew any hint of male chauvinism and accept the fact that the rapidly responsive penis is more often a result of male anxiety, specifically referential to women. Premature ejaculation is never experienced during masturbation, and it is an almost unheard of complaint among homosexuals. It is an exclusively male complaint, since most women, if they do climax before their obliging partner, remain capable and happy to continue until their male companion's satisfaction is assured.

Habitual prematurity is the cry of a distressed penis, and its possessor should seek psychiatric aid rather than Kinsey's questionable comforture.

Hosts of beleaguered penises have defensively sought asylum in apathy. It appears that the male's emotional estrangement from the erotic is rapidly assuming protean proportions. It is becoming increasingly common to hear women complain of the sexual coldness, distance, and indifference of their dates, lovers, and mates. In a typical survey of college-educated young wives, 69 percent were satisfied with the frequency of their sexual relations, 6 percent found them "too frequent," while 25 percent complained of the infrequency of their marital relations. The fact that one in four women, at least in this study, found their mates relatively disinterested in sex is no small complaint, and echos what most psychiatrists are hearing in their consultation rooms. Penile performance is apparently becoming perfunctory. It is a moot point to what extent these complaints are Eve's seeking an ecstatic return to an amorous Eden, or how much they are attributable to the overwhelming of the male psyche. Probably both are true. Increased female expectations and demands are countered by increased indifference and detachment, the opening gambits in the apathetic alternative. The recent emphasis on being "cool," promulgated by the contemporary youth culture, has aided in freezing male responsivity. One finds the apathetic penis among young men who hide from involvement and affection. As they age, partake in sequential monogamy, or finally marry, their sex lives tend to become mechanized, devoid of variation, surprise, or innovation. Saturday night genital approximations, ritualized pelvic motions, become as routinized as taking the 7:10 commuter train on Monday morning. They are frequently less enjoyable. Stimulation becomes a dimly remembered recollection of things past, occasionally revived by a lithesome secretary or by a flirtatious gesture emanating from someone else's wife. The recreational penis now becomes preoccupied with urination. The fact that men and other humans were neither destined nor effectively programmed for a monogamous existence is lost sight of by a social order which fosters the myth of "and they lived happily ever after." As monotony envelops monogamy, both partners slowly drift apart toward opposite sides of the bed. Passionate play, in some respects, is not unlike a football game. The same play, repeated over and over again, results in an impregnable defense. The constant invention of new plays, or a successful and well-timed mix of the old, adds to a team's variety and increases its scoring potential.

The vulnerability of the male member is most graphically demonstrated by its withdrawal into perpetual detumescence. Impotency is the state of the ostensibly palsied penis, which cannot erect or sufficiently maintain an erection to permit intercourse to occur. There is no commandment stating that a penis must perform each time, under all circumstances, and with every female it happens to encounter. Most penises have their occasional understandable lapses, and so its anxious possessor should not diagnose impotency based on a single or an occasional happenstance. It is habitual nonresponsiveness which is the hallmark of impotency.

While statistics are readily available quantifying the prevalence of influenza, divorce, heart disease, and unemployment in men, there is no agency that collects data on the incidence of impotency. Yet it is probably the case that impotency has become the least publicized epidemic of the past decade. This impression is gleaned from my patients, both male and female, from articles appearing in medical journals, and from conversations with my colleagues. Kinsey's study of male sexuality in the 1940s reported erectile impotence in 1.3 percent in men below age thirty-five. In a 1970 poll conducted by a popular magazine, *Psychology Today*, more than one in every three responding males was having erectile difficulties. While this questionnaire only reached a selected group of respondents, and consequently may have been skewed toward those likely to have a problem or two, it is highly unlikely that the impotency rate today is anywhere near the low level reported by Kinsey. Either Kinsey erred, or impotency has secretly soared in the past twenty years.

Impotency results from a multitude of stresses exerted

on the penis, arising from any one of a multitude of causes. Physical illness, diseases such as diabetes, thyroid insufficiency, multiple sclerosis, to mention a few, are rare although possible etiological factors. Drug intake is a somewhat more common cause. Shakespeare's observation that alcohol "provokes the desire, but takes away the performance" is as astute a medical observation as would be found in any textbook. Italian ladies of the Renaissance used a drug which dilated the pupils of their eyes, converting them into deep, darkened pools of passion. The drug was called "belladonna," since it made women more beautiful. Belladonna derivatives are used in many over-the-counter sedatives today, purchasable without a prescription. While they continue to exert their hypnotic effects, excess dosages may deflate sensitive penises. Heroin is also noteworthy for making men less horny. But these, and other drug-induced penile insufficiencies, are relatively rare and disappear once the noxious agent is dispensed with.

It was once thought that a low level of penile erectability was associated with a low level of testosterone in the blood, especially in older men. But this has proven to be just one more blind alley, for the therapeutic administration of testosterone usually has little or no effect on the impotent penis. Even the administration of clomiphene, a drug which doubles the testosterone level to higher than normal, has proven a failure with most chronically impotent men. Some male homosexuals with low testosterone levels are exceedingly sexually active, with no erectile difficulties. Apparently the penis requires only a minimal amount of testosterone for successful operation, and the somewhat lower levels in older men may indicate little more than sexual apathy, a lack of opportunity, or the absence of a stimulating and available partner.

By all odds, the most common *agent provocateur* is a

conflicted psyche. Orgasmic dysfunction is the brain's ultimate veto over the penis.

Psychologically-induced impotency is a problem-solving device employed by the brain to the chagrin of the penis. Its psychic origin is announced by the occurrence of an erection under any circumstances in addition to the familiar ones. A physically-incapacitated phallus never erects. Awakening with an erection, the retention of a masturbatory capability, or the presence of an enlarging phallus with women other than the accustomed one all point to a problem residing above the neck rather than below the navel.

The havoc within the copulaphobic male arises from sets of conflicting themes. Exaggerated images of masculinity meet expectations of limited capacities; conscious desire for female contact conflicts with hidden hostility toward, or fear of, one, some, or all women; antisexual childhood conditioning confronts the erotic imperatives of adulthood; the search for physical pleasure abuts against imaginary fears of punishment and genital injury. The themes are legion but, with the penis remaining limp, the anxiety-laden copulation is avoided.

Project yourself. After months of hesitation, you finally find yourself in Dr. Freud's office. Fidgeting in your chair, you confront a reasonably pleasant and interested man, not quite the stereotype you've seen in the magazine cartoons, who asks what the problem is. You've rehearsed this interview dozens of times in the last several days. How does one express the problem? "I seem to have developed some sexual inadequacy." No. It sounds too technical, too impersonal. "I can't seem to get it up the way I used to." Again, no. It has a crass ring to it. "If I get a hard-on, I lose it before . . ." You begin to feel a bit ridiculous. "Look, I've become impotent." There, it's out, and he doesn't appear noticeably shocked or taken aback. Why should he, he's been hearing it often enough.

"When did it start?"

"I'm really not sure. I know that I've been less interested in sex for some time, but I dismissed it as a passing phase. And then it just seemed to happen. At first I couldn't hold an erection, and then I couldn't have one at all."

"At all?"

"Not quite. I frequently wake up with an erection, and I can masturbate, but when I get into bed with her, no dice."

"How do you feel about it?"

Somehow you had not anticipated that question. Your first reaction is distress and devastation. You're impotent, you're ashamed, you're incapacitated and functionally crippled, yet all of you, to be truthful, is not unhappy about it. There is a feeling of relief, a relaxation of pressure.

As treatment progresses, you find that you aren't a self-pitying, whining Alexander Portnoy, but simply a man using a symptom, impotency, to express "I've had it!" Striving toward a chimera of success for insufficient reasons, bored with a demanding wife or lover you've become emotionally estranged from years before, feeling yourself aging and wasting your allotted time with little in the way of satisfaction, you have symbolically copped out. No more performing, you're crippled. "Don't expect too much from me, I'm limited." In one fell swoop you have expressed your rage and reduced the demands. Small wonder that part of you secretly cherishes and clings to the symptom.

Prognostically, your chances of recovery are quite good. A change in the way you conceptualize yourself and the rest of your world may be called for, but the odds are that you will end up happier, and hopefully so will your lady friend.

A man need not endure the anxiety attendant to premature ejaculation nor the despair of copulaphobia to withdraw from the sexual encounter. He may propel his penis through the appropriate and properly paced motions, all the while concentrating on nonsexual concerns. Beneath the facade of sexual activity, a man might seek reassurance that he is something other than the inferior being he conceives himself to be, or he might, for those few moments, temporarily escape from pervasive gnawings of aloneness and alienation.

Sex may become an expression of hostility, with each penile thrust regarded as an assaultive "fuck you." Some men are at their coital best only after a battle with their partner, with what passes for "sexual" activity serving as the final round of the fight. Rape, that supposed epitome of male lust, is fundamentally an attack, albeit one which happens to be acted out within the sexual sphere by men who are plagued by their own masculine inadequacies. A pretty twenty-year-old teacher in a suburban public school was forced from her classroom at knifepoint by an intruder who had only moments ago robbed another female teacher. The attacker demanded money. When she showed him her empty purse, he abducted and raped her, his penis symbolically stabbing her again and again, in frustrated fury. The motive was attack, the tool was his penis.

The drive for power and control ofttimes converts the playground of the bed into a phantasmal battlefield. "Good grief, I can actually turn her on?!" is incredulously reexperienced by insecure men impressed and overwhelmed by the awesome power inherent in actually affecting another human being. Men who turn limp at the sight of their partner happily hovering above them in bed are generally men who have been more concerned with the affirmation of their power and control than with sexual delectation. Fellatio, instead of being regarded as a sensual aperitif, becomes stimulating only by virtue of assumed female submissiveness and complementary cunnilingus is shunned lest it connote male inferiority. Prior to the sexual revolution, it was by no means uncommon for women to manipulate their males by granting or withholding sexual favors. Its popular translation was: "If he doesn't come across, I don't come across." With the sexual balance swinging in the opposite direction, men are beginning to utilize the same device, to the frustration of their frantic wives or girl friends.

The detached and alienated male may find his one source of human contact through his penis. Unable to emotionally communicate with others of his species, the sexual act affords some semblance of a relationship with another human being. The wife of a successful engineer who found herself unable to control perpetual rages with tranquilizing medication was referred for psychiatric treatment by her family physician. These outbursts were directed primarily against her husband, with her small children serving as secondary targets. The problem centered around her husband's uncommunicability. A detached and dehumanized automaton, he seldom uttered a "hello" in the evening nor a "goodbye" in the morning. Arriving home each night, renewed by his latest triumph over a blueprint, he ate his dinner and majestically retired to his den to "work" or to contemplate the state of the world. His only attempt at relatedness evidenced itself in bed. His distraught wife was "to adore his penis" by giving him a "good blow job," and was to be available for "a good fuck" at a moment's notice, often during television commercials. Unable to communicate with her husband, and welded to children too young to communicate with on any level above the sandbox, her understandable explosivity was only defused by an eventual divorce. Her next husband proved to be a warm and verbal human being. To date, they are living happily ever after. Her ex-husband continues his love affair with his penis and his television set, still unable to comprehend how his infantile fantasies of omnipotence failed him.

When a male's early sexual development has been so devastated that future sexual contacts are perceived as sufficiently threatening, he may unconsciously but understandably develop a sexually deviant orientation. Exhibitionism, fetishism, transvestism, sado-masochism, bestiality, and pedophilia (attraction to children) are some of the possibilities. Homosexuality might also be considered within this framework.

Through these deviations the psyche attempts to preserve some measure of sexual gratification, while evading the fantasied spectre of frightening consequences (castration, annihilation, and other such unpleasantries) attendant to the more conventional coital activities. While these "alternatives" are a commentary on a male's sexual fragility, they are also a tribute to his adaptive potentials. Residing almost exclusively within the male domain, they are seldom found in women, whose sexuality appears to be founded on sterner foundations. Kinsey reported only two or three cases of female fetishists, no female exhibitionists (those who impulsively display their genitals to the opposite sex and derive sexual gratification thereof), and only one-third the percentage of sado-masochistic responses when compared with male reactions. There are thought to be twice as many male homosexuals as there are lesbians.

While the uterus and vagina relax, contemplating their creative potentials, the deviant phallus portrays the pounded boxer, the pugilist on the ropes, battered and covering up, weaving and dodging the real and imagined blows raining in upon him. Above all, he must avoid his adversary. And so the fetishistic phallus is aroused only by inanimate objects (shoes, clothing) or by only a part of the body (feet, toes). "Fetishism" is derived from the Portuguese *feitico*, a charm, with the penis responding to the amulet, to a symbol rather than to a real person. The transvestite achieves gratification simply from wearing female attire, as if women's dress will disguise the existence of a penis, thus warding off some dire genital threat. While women in drag may derive some satisfaction in male mimicry, a penile fantasy is not involved, and they seldom, if ever, become orgastic because of their attire. The masochist confronts the imagined assault in a more direct fashion, by symbolically incorporating the anticipated punishment for sexual pleasure into the act itself. In a sense, the masochist preempts the executioner by accepting punishment in advance, thus allowing orgasm to take place. Leopold von Sacher-Masoch, a nineteenth-century Austrian novelist, would entreat his wife, Wanda, to whip and beat him as a prelude to sexual relations. Wanda courteously obliged, and Sacher-Masoch was immortalized in the term "masochism" as the epitome of suffering and humiliation in the pursuit of sexual gratification. Men have extended this bizarre erotic passion play to the point of deliberately placing themselves in life-threatening situations, with nooses tied around their necks, passively submitting to being burned with lighted cigarettes or being beaten with metal clothes hangers to the point of unconsciousness. Others have pushed the play too far, ending up on a slab in the morgue rather than in sexual ecstasy.

## The Once and Future Penis

Proclamations announcing the permanent demise of the penis as a power within the arena of sexual politics may yet prove to be premature. While the penile position is apparently at its nadir, its capacity to adapt to changing circumstances has been evidenced in the past. A phoenix rising from its ashes, an Arthur who once was, and in the future will again be, *hic jacet penis Rex quondam Rexque futurus*, the phallic comeback is eagerly awaited by a generation of perplexed males, and by more than a few women as well.

The restoration of the penis to a respectable social position will require an innovative sexual renaissance that reaches beyond instruction manuals and somber manifestos to the realm of relaxation and humor. The currently enshrined sacred cows, the cult of erotic aestheticism, the "equality" of male and female sexuality, the masculine role of initiation and of technical proficiency, the female's right to define the male as a success or a failure as a sensual animal, all call for a quizzical wink.

While other bodily functions have little in the way of the mystical attached to them, human sexuality has been accorded a unique distinction. The Olympian heights of relational sex, represented as a divine spasm in which the human race transcends itself, is beyond the capacities and aspirations of many an adequate penis. Let us redefine sex on a more physiological and less spiritual level, as a shared playful escapade rather than a transcendental experience of "Beauty" and "Sanctity." Social groups that are relatively free of this "spiritual" necessity regard sex as a natural process, no more aesthetic than any other bodily activity. Sexual intertwinings, couplings, and contortions are exciting and pleasurable, but describing them, or the

intensely felt summation of stimuli, as aesthetically beautiful or spiritually significant would appear to be semantic
acrobatics. The freedom to be simply and unencumberedly
sensual is the least a penis can ask of society.

A gentle reappraisal of the male role in sexual relations would be appreciated by most penises. The assumptions are made that the male is always sexually available,
his penis aching to erect on a moment's notice with but
the slightest provocation; that he should and will restrain
himself as long as his mate deems it necessary; and that
he will somehow induce the orgasm to which his partner
in her current enlightenment is unquestionably entitled.
There is a pervasive taint of inequity in this arrangement.
The onus placed upon the male is vast, while the female's
responsibilities are relatively minimal. One survey of sex
manuals indicated that men were the recipients of three
to four times as many instructions as were women. It
would seem that these eroticized versions of *Popular
Mechanics* were geared to the production of computer-
ized, automatized phalluses, programmed to please their
mates rather than to enhance their own responses, since
the cock crows earlier than the hen. Women are consequently forced into the role of judges who define the
success or the failure of their male partners. Since some
studies show 30 percent of American women are non-
orgastic, and furthermore, with the exception of premature ejaculation, there is little clinical evidence that the
male's technique actually determines whether or not a
woman reaches her moment of fruition, the man and his
penis become the victims of a subtle form of sexual discrimination and oppression. The male has been anointed
as the purveyor of sexual delight and gratification to
womankind, and there is nothing to suggest that he vol-
unteered for the job. I have listened to numerous men
describing themselves perspiring in the all-too-common

overly extended erotic embrace, their penises having despaired of the opportunity for a natural and spontaneous orgasm, their minds concentrating on the multiplication tables or the horrors of the following day at the office to calm their insistent penises, mechanically thrusting in and out to induce their partners to finally utter that blessed word "Come." Excitation gives way to mechanization, sex becomes work, and the high-spirited penis is dulled and dispassionate.

Men must transfer more responsibility to women for their own moments of ecstasy. It should be incumbent upon both men and women to communicate their sexual wants and preferences to their partner. What type of foreplay is most enjoyable? Should clitoral stimulation be direct or indirect? Does lingual, anal, or priapic stimulations turn her on or shut her off? How much intercourse does he or she prefer? If a woman's requirements are conveyed, and are congenial, it is only reasonable for the male to comply. Should her needs be unstated, insatiable, or subject to change without notice, the woman should have the fundamental humanity to accept the problem as her own and encourage her partner to cease his superhuman efforts and to comfortably and relaxedly ejaculate. Freed of the imperative to "satisfy" and more relaxed in its consequent performance, the penis should become more prolific and less prone to future potency problems. Indeed, the best insurance against impotency is an active sex life plus the availability of a physically and emotionally healthy partner.

The penile resurrection will regard the notion of sexual "equality" as both artificial and absurd. There are more inequitable situations in life than there are equitable ones, and the concept of "fairness" is more often honored in the breach than in the observance. There are differences in the sexual responsiveness of men and women, both individually and collectively. Tastes, expectations, and performances differ. The simultaneous orgasm has been established as the male's diploma, a certification that he has received his Ph.D. in Passionate Play. Yet simultaneity is by no means the norm, and, considering the difference in male and female responses, it might best be regarded as a pleasant artifact. Instead of the responsibility for sexual regulation and satisfaction devolving upon one partner, it should be a joint venture worked out as harmoniously and hedonistically as possible by both participants. Given a sufficiently adventuresome attitude, most men and women can experience more than a modicum of satiety without recourse to manuals or gurus of technique.

The male initiatory role must also be regarded as passé and quietly go the way of the mastodon. Why must the insecure male, or the male who is made anxious by assertive behavior, make each and every advance? A major technique employed by the sex clinics, for example, has been the assigning of the initiatory role to women. They straddle the male during intercourse, better controlling the interaction and taking greater responsibility for it; they squeeze the premature penis to control the early ejaculation; and they initiate sexual activity by stroking and touching. Whatever degree of success the sex clinics have achieved, the relaxation of imperative pressures upon the male must be given its share of the credit. Historically, many cultures have found no difficulty in allowing for female initiatory behavior; why not encourage its normalcy within ours? It apparently has a beneficial effect on both sexes.

The concept of the impetuously erectile penis is an additional candidate for oblivion. While the seventeen- or eighteen-year-old penis is hot-blooded and likely to be on the move, he finds sex less immediate with age, and is content with fewer orgasms. Some men fear this normal change of pace as a reflection of diminished virility. Panic sets in and they become candidates for impotency or sexual apathy. They might better compare themselves with a veteran baseball pitcher who no longer relies on speed but has become a master of pace and control; his wildness gone, he throws fewer but better-placed pitches.

The epilogue to the saga of penile salvation can only be written when the penis has been rescued from the Mystique. The Sexual Athlete has played overly long and his contract should be terminated. Sex will then be recognized as amateur recreation rather than a crucible. If a man insists on "proving himself," let it be in an area other than the bedroom. With the decline of the Mystique's imperatives, with a bill of divorcement from grandiose penile pretensions a *fait accompli*, men will view their appendages in human terms, and so will women. Then the fun will begin.

# 5

# The Homosexual "Alternative"

*Homosexuality is assuredly no advantage,*
*but it is nothing to be ashamed of. . . .*
                              SIGMUND FREUD

YOU ARE INVITED to dinner in Limbo, a unique event which allegedly occurs at least once in each man's eternity. Seated at a table in the dining room are Leonardo da Vinci, Julius Caesar, Plato, Tschaikovsky, and Walt Whitman. A rather heterogeneous group; you wonder what they might conceivably have in common. The conversation is sparked by Leonardo ruefully reflecting upon his imprisonment in Florence on charges of homosexuality, and Caesar commenting on his reputation as "the husband of every woman, and the wife of every man." Potential dining companions with similar inclinations might include Michelangelo, Sappho, Marlowe, and innumerable persons of talent and repute whose homosexual predilections have understandably been hidden in their respective closets. Since homosexuals have been beheaded, castrated, burned, imprisoned, disgraced, assaulted, blackmailed, and forced to suicide as a result of their supposed "crime against nature," the advertising of one's sexual deviation has always appeared a gallant although rash enterprise. Shunned and ostracized as social pariahs, it is small wonder that so little information has been gathered about the etiology and life styles of men and women whose sexual preferences are for those of their own sex.

But times and customs do change. Perhaps it began in 1935, with Freud's letter to an American mother who had requested his assistance for her homosexual son. In his now famous reply, Freud wrote, in part, "Homosexuality is assuredly no advantage, but it is nothing to be ashamed of, no vice, no degradation. . . ." This was followed by statistical revelations, such as the Kinsey reports of the late 1940s and early 1950s, which announced that 4 percent of adult white American males and 2 percent of white American women lead exclusively homosexual lives. If we add the 10 percent who have been exclusively homosexual for at least three years between their mid-teens and mid-fifties, this predominantly homosexual group would be large enough to populate Detroit, Philadelphia, Los Angeles, Houston, Washington, D.C., plus a substantial assortment of other smaller cities. While these numbers may not be as wide as the Shakespearean church door, nor as deep as a well, they were enough to make an impact on American social consciousness. Previously unmentionable in the public press, homosexuality became increasingly suitable matter for the various news media and stage and television plays. Research into the homosexual condition became increasingly "respectable." A grant request was submitted to the National Institute of Mental Health in Washington, D.C., in 1960 entitled "The Etiology of Female Homosexuality." It was returned with a change in title. The new title read "The Etiology of Female Deviancy." Happily the atmosphere is changing, for the same National Institute of Mental Health has recently established a group devoted to the investigation of homosexuality, and the Kinsey-established Institute for Sex Research has finally been granted funds to pursue research in the homosexual area, after being turned down by twenty-five private foundations. Their findings are eagerly awaited, for they represent the first mass-research approach to the question of homosexuality since mankind began its sexual experimentations thousands of years ago.

The rise in public concern over civil liberties, coupled with the current revolution in sexual mores, focused further attention on the homosexual condition. Homosexual organizations, established in the 1950s, are currently increasing in numbers and in influence. The male Mattachine Society was incorporated in California in 1953. The name "Mattachine" was deliberately selected for its obscurity. The original Mattachines were professional entertainers and advisers to the Italian nobility notable for their truthful approach in the face of the unpleasant consequences that might ensue should their predictions prove faulty. The female counterpart of the Mattachine Society was the Daughters of Bilitis, "a woman's organization for the purpose of promoting the integration of the homosexual into society." The name is derived from *The Songs of Bilitis* by Pierre Louys, in which the supposedly heterosexual Bilitis becomes a disciple of Sappho and lesbian love. While the original purposes of these and similar organizations were to educate the public about homosexuality and to assist the adjustment of the homosexual within his society, in the past few years there is a new militancy on the part of many homophiles.

The homosexual counterpart of the Boston Tea Party was the "Stonewall Rebellion." Police and legal harassment had been an onerous but tacitly "accepted" part of the life of the active homosexual. Raids on places of congregation, primarily "gay bars," had become an expected and wretched commonplace of existence. In June of 1969, a routine raid was visited upon the Stonewall Inn, a Greenwich Village bar frequented by a substantial homosexual clientele. Instead of the typically pacific parade into the waiting paddy wagons, the customers revolted, pelting the police with bottles, stones, and other missiles. Police reinforcements were called and the riot quelled, but the issue had been joined. Various militant homosexual groups united under the banner of the Gay Liberation Front and public action became the order of the day. The original educative and self-help activities directed at obtaining legal and social acceptance for homosexuals were replaced by demands for full "equality" with heterosexuals on a social and cultural basis, plus the promulgation of homosexuality as an "alternative" and possibly "preferable" life style to heterosexuality for both men and women.

It is this homosexual "alternative" which is presently being presented to the male, already neck deep in the struggle to deal with the burgeoning complexities of his role in our society. An offer is tendered to eschew the conventional male role, to divest himself of many of its demands, and to embrace the alternative instead. To those whose sexual identities are not firmly fixed, to those who feel in a state of flux, the offer has the seductive quality of a Siren's Song.

A major tremor in the current erotic earthquake has been the acute questioning of previously held values, assumptions, and definitions. What is meant by "homosexual"? Should a man or a woman be exclusively heterosexual? Is bisexuality the biological norm, and the heterosexual just kidding himself? Is homosexuality a less stressful and more preferable life style? Does an isolated or occasional sexual dream, experience, or fantasy involving another of the same sex denote a "homosexual"? Do

the group masturbatory experiences of early adolescence
or the sexual relations which take place in prisons or on
board ships connote sexual "deviance"? For simplicity's
sake, the following might be an operating definition: A
homosexual is any adult who is preferentially aroused by,
and who engages in repetitive sexual activities with,
members of his or her own sex. This definition would
exclude those who partake in "situational" homosexual
relationships, such as prisoners, since heterosexual activities are not available. It would additionally exclude that
cluster of men whose dependency and assertive needs
incline them to identify with those perceived as more
powerful and competent. Since they are basically very
frightened and insecure heterosexuals, eventually desir-
ous of a successful relationship with women, they tend to
rely on other men to provide them with the wherewithal
to succeed. The man who is immersed in homoerotic
fantasy, however, although sexually inactive, perhaps
should be considered homosexual. One would first want
to know what it is that he seeks in his fantasy life and the
reason for his celibacy before making any commitment
concerning his basic sexual orientation. The definition
excludes the concept of the "latent homosexual" as an
imprecise idea which has given far more confusion than
aid.

Both implicitly and explicitly the homosexual activist
challenges the traditional presumption that homosexuality is "abnormal." While attempting to present the various
points of view, obviously I have my own, though neither
I nor anyone else has the "Final Answer" at the present
time. Suppositions range from the thesis that the homosexual is superior to his or her heterosexual counterpart
through the more conventional postulation of some type
of "disorder." A positional spectrum from the extreme left
to the conservative right can be discerned:

## I. The "Ultimate Solution"

The "Ultimate Solution," which appeals only to a few extremists, holds that the opposite sex should simply be abolished or exterminated. This position is propounded by Valerie Solanas in her *S.C.U.M. Manifesto* (S.C.U.M. = Society for Cutting Up Men), wherein maleness is defined as a "deficiency disease." Since the male is seen as "incapable of empathizing or identifying with others, of love, friendship, affection, or tenderness . . . there remains to civic minded, responsible, thrill-seeking females only to overthrow the government, eliminate the money system, institute complete automation and destroy the male sex." Since she sees the male as "an emotional parasite and, therefore, not ethically entitled to live," Miss Solanas finds "the elimination of any male . . . a righteous and good act." In accordance with her philosophy, she shot Andy Warhol. Although Miss Solanas does appeal to some women, and is quoted sympathetically by Germaine Greer in *The Female Eunuch* and other feminist writers as well, I as a male find it rather impossible to discuss this position from an unbiased point of view, except to note that I question its practical utility.

## II. "Gay Is Better"

This position is perhaps best presented by the slogans heard and seen at activists' conclaves, such as "Try it, you'll like it," or "Peter Pan is a lesbian," or the chant "Two, four, six, eight, being gay is better than being straight." Some radical lesbians, also known as "Radishes," have a Marxist orientation and advocate political revolution as a necessary component of an overall sexual revolution. The radical homosexual maintains that the homophile relationship is more satisfying personally and sexually than a heterosexual liaison. This viewpoint is popularized with the implication that homosexuality is the nobler and more desirable way of life, "a perfect answer to the population explosion." From the sexual standpoint, many homosexuals maintain that a person of the same sex is best equipped and able to understand the sexual responses of his or her own sex, and is consequently in a better position to gratify. Let me here quote Miss Greer vis-à-vis the claims of feminist lesbians: "At all events, a clitoral orgasm with a full cunt is nicer than a clitoral orgasm with an empty one, as far as I can tell at least. Besides, a man is more than a dildo."

## III. A Normal Variance

The assumption is made that homosexuality is merely a statistical departure from the norm. Consequently, it is no more deviant than a red-haired individual in a predominantly brunette society, or a left-handed golfer in a shop filled with right-handed clubs. This stance was dramatically stated when a group of thirty homosexual activists broke into a meeting of the American Psychiatric Association in the spring of 1971 and commandeered the podium. Their leader excoriated the two thousand psychiatrists in the audience with: "We are here to denounce your authority to call us sick or mentally disordered. . . ."

Precisely what is meant by "sickness" or "disorder"? Is homosexuality an "illness" in the medical sense, or is it rather a "difference" which our culture erroneously labels "sick" because it doesn't conform to the accepted societal standards? Since some homosexuals feel satisfied with their lives and appear as well adjusted or as equally problemed as the average heterosexual, any connotation of "abnormality" on other than a purely statistical basis is fought. If, on the other hand, one assumes that heterosexuality is "obviously" the natural mode of development in all animal species, it follows that the homosexual has somehow been deflected from the normal developmental path. Furthermore, this "deviant" adaptation would still be aberrant regardless of the response of any particular society. The issue of *our* particular societal prejudice is of questionable validity in this context since, with the exception of ancient Greece and pre-Meiji Japan, homosexuality has been regarded as deviant in all but a few minor subcultures. Even the Greeks distinguished a socially sanctioned "pederasty," a love of boys, from the homosexual life, which was much less esteemed. While the label of "deviancy" may be nothing more than a manifestation of historical ignorance, it may equally reflect the collective wisdom of generations. The lines are sharply drawn, but the question has only been resolved in minds already closed.

A variant of the approach that homosexuality is a normal variance, frequently heard within organized homosexual groups, goes something like this: "We don't think of the homosexual as 'sick,' but even if he was, he can't be helped by any form of treatment, so leave us alone." While no sane psychiatrist advocates the mandatory treatment of anyone by psychoanalysis or other therapeutic techniques, simply because he or she is homosexual, this rigidity in approach only hampers the rational consideration of the entire subject of homosexuality.

## IV. *"Born Homosexual"*

A tempting hypothesis is that homosexuality is the result of expression of some inherent biological abnormality, genetic or hormonal. The effeminate male homosexual, the "queen," and the masculine-appearing lesbian, the "butch" or "dyke," make the onlooker wonder whether they are indeed physically the same as other members of their sex. The overwhelming majority of homosexuals of both sexes, however, cannot be distinguished as such by even the most sophisticated of observers, including other homosexuals.

Much research remains to be done in this embryonic area. There are some hints to suggest that men with an extra X chromosome in their genetic makeup retain a heterosexual orientation, and women with an XO (only one X chromosome) chromosomal pattern, although evidencing some physical differences from other women, retain their heterosexual proclivities. One study of homosexual twins had suggested a genetic predisposition, but these findings have been seriously questioned, and other studies of monozygotic (identical) twins in which one was homosexual and the other heterosexual seem to refute the genetic theory. Yet there may be genetic factors still unidentified. For example, homosexuals tend to be born later in the sibling chain than would be expected on a statistical basis. They are more often the youngest, or near the youngest, of their brothers or sisters. While this might only reflect a close-binding relatedness to a mother whose sexual life with her husband has waned with the years, inducing her to seek emotional gratification from her "baby," it might also be one more situation in which subtle chromosomal changes occur with aging parents which are then passed on to their offspring.

Animal studies, both pre- and postnatal, with injections of varied sexual hormones at critical stages of development have been intriguing but inconclusive. A Los Angeles study in April of 1971 reported abnormalities in the breakdown products of testosterone in twelve of fifteen male homosexuals. However, similar findings were observed in four male heterosexuals who were in poor health. Variations in the urinary steroids of four female homosexuals were also reported. In November 1971, researchers in another study in St. Louis reported the finding of lower blood levels of the male sex hormone, testosterone, in young men who were exclusively or predominantly homosexual. It could not be determined whether the hormonal differences represented a causative factor or were the consequence of homosexual behavior and its attendant stresses. These same researchers noted that previous attempts to "cure" homosexuality by the administration of testosterone only increased the person's sexual drive rather than altering its direction. The numbers of people utilized in these studies were not very large, and the findings are not specific for homosexuality, but there is the suggestion of some hormonal factor at work in at least the partial etiology of some instances of homosexuality. It may eventually prove to be the case that some prenatal hormonal event is a significant predisposing factor. Consider the possibility that there may be a deficiency in the quality or the quantity of the male sex hormones during that portion of the life of the fetus during which the sexual responsivity centers of the brain are being "masculinized." Might this produce a tendency toward later responsivity to the same sex, while not interfering with the obvious anatomical development of the male? It works this way in experimental animals. Might it not be the case with some human beings? Further substantiation is awaited, since dozens of hormonal theories have been promulgated in the past, at least as far back as 1892, only to be subsequently discarded. The response of the president of the Los Angeles Mattachine Society, Franklin Kameny, Ph.D., to these studies as "no more relevant to the real problems of homosexuals than the biochemistry of melanin is to blacks" is both poignant and regettable. An eminent jurist once commented that the beginning of wisdom is the suspension of judgment.

## V. "A Family Affair"

The "Nature versus Nurture" controversy is an intellectual plague which has infested mankind with an "either-or" type of rational rigor mortis. Whether manifested in the educational field, race relations, childhood development, or homosexuality, the controversy encourages men to prematurely take rigid positions. Is homosexuality inherent in the individual, or are we dealing with a phenomenon engendered by environmental forces exacting their inexorable toll upon the individual as he or she develops? The various biological conceptions of homosexuality previously discussed generally fall under the "Nature" category. The theory of the experiential induction of homosexuality stresses the influence of environmental experiences, over and above the "nature" one is born with. Most clinical psychiatrists tend to embrace this position after becoming acquainted with the life histories of homosexuals. When confronted with intimate data, especially details of family interrelationships, it is difficult to see how the individual could have developed in any other direction. But then, there are always the exceptions...

The classic description of the family constellation most often associated with the production of male homosexuality was formulated by Irving Bieber and his associates in 1962. Based on the premise that heterosexuality is the biological norm and that homosexuality is most probably the consequence of some environmental inhibition of normal heterosexual development, a postulation was made that specific family constellations might be ascertained which would most likely result in homosexuality. Close examination of the family backgrounds of 106 male homosexuals undergoing psychoanalytic treatment seemed to provide just such a constellation.

It was found that a family with a close-binding, overly-intimate, and seductive mother, conjoined with a detached and hostile father, provided fertile soil for the development of homosexuality in a son. This typical mother dominates and demeans her husband, who often appears as a hostile intruder within the family. The destructive interaction between the parents is focused on a particular son, who then becomes the victim of his parents' pathology. Caught in a bind between his mother's closeness and seductiveness and his father's hostility and distance, the boy must renounce his heterosexual strivings in his own self-defense. Identification and relationships with other men then become in a sense reparative, allowing for sexual expression but in a fashion that reduces the threat inherent in heterosexual activities. Since sexual play with women is generally evocative of anxiety, there is a frequent fear of, and an aversion to, the female genitalia. Heterosexual impotency may reflect a man's fear of real or symbolic castration as a punishment for his closeness to his mother, or her overpossessiveness may be so overwhelming that other women inspire the *vagina dentata* (the vagina with teeth) fantasy in which a man imagines the loss of his penis in a toothed vagina.

In most circumstances, the boy is attached to a mother

who infantilizes him and discourages a free assertion and development of his masculinity, while at the same time he is deprived of an adequate father figure to identify with. An involved and loving father is rarer than a dinosaur egg in the families of male homosexuals. As a boy matures, he finds himself cut off from a supportive and encouraging group of peers. Feeling himself an outsider, a loner, and "queer," he naturally gravitates to others on the periphery, if they are available. Sooner or later, contact is made with someone more homosexually committed and a tentative resolution to his conflicts is found. Once introduced into the "gay scene," a more stable and accepting environment is available and his homosexual identification becomes more fixed.

A further reinforcement for the environmental etiology of homosexuality was a similar investigation in 1967 of twenty-four female homosexuals. Again, a fairly typical family constellation emerged, in which the father appeared to play the stellar role. A composite picture of this father portrayed a man who appeared puritanical, yet manifested a seductive attitude toward his frightened daughter only slightly below the surface. He was overly possessive, attempting to exclude the mother, as well as friends, both male and female, from intimacy with his daughter. Excessively interested in her physical development, he simultaneously frowned upon her play with dolls, use of cosmetics, and other aspects of her growing female identification. In short, he discouraged her emergence as a functioning female. The image of a close-binding overly intimate father mirrored the close-binding intimate mother found in the studies of male homosexuality.

A somewhat different family constellation was ascertained in a later study of twenty-five homosexual girls in the New York City public school system, girls primarily from the lower socio-economic group. The fathers of this group were characterized as "hostile, exploitative, detached, and absent," while the mothers appeared overburdened and unable to deal with their family responsibilities. These mothers often conveyed negative attitudes toward men to their daughters. Family constellations do indeed induce homosexuality, but apparently more than one specific familial configuration is involved.

Once an individual has identified himself as a homosexual, he is impelled to make some social adjustment to it. The homosexual world, like the rest of society, is divided into several subcultures, and the subculture entered depends on one's personality makeup, luck, and the circumstances which his particular milieu affords.

Relatively few homosexuals settle down permanently with one special partner. The majority, however, cut off from the heterosexual world around them, frequently seek multiple relationships in an effort to achieve a sense of belonging as well as the satisfaction of various emotional requisites. The popular conception of a pseudo male-female type of relationship does not generally stand up under close scrutiny. There is more a sharing of congenial role activities in life, both in and out of bed. Unfortunately, unconscious or dimly perceived needs of the partner are infrequently met, and, consequently, the break-up of these partnerships is more the rule than the exception. The substitute father or mother figure, the elusive tower of strength, understanding, and support, is rarely equal to the assignment. Since each partner has needs of his own, stormy and hostile dissolutions are frequent. There are those fortunate few who make the adjustment, and their accomplishment, under great societal pressures and disapproval, should not be taken lightly.

The majority of homosexuals find themselves in stressful and emotionally isolated life situations. The common homosexual experience is the continual "cruise," a constant excursion into the world of gay bars, public baths, men's rooms, and other public meeting places in which encounters occur, evaluations are made, and assignations established. Dr. Evelyn Hooker, a psychologist who has extensively studied the homosexual population of California, describes the gay bar as serving as "an induction, training, and integration center" for those entering the gay life. The habitués of these various establishments are quite eager and willing to initiate the homosexual tenderfoot into the rules of the game and the facts of homosexual life. They are instructed in the variety of sexual activities, the wonders of the one-night or ten-minute stand in which a sexual relationship is deliberately transacted in a starkly impersonal manner. Bodily contact without pretense of interpersonal commitment or attachment is the rule. Person-to-person is replaced by genital-to-genital. Novices are taught the nuances of gesture, the eyeball-to-eyeball invitation, and special non-verbal communications which signal interest and availability. There is emphasis on youth, attractiveness, and "well-hung" genitals. Glibness and repartee replace deeper conversation. Of course this is rather rough on the aging homosexual, whose physical and social attributes are no longer assets. He becomes the exploited purchaser of sexual services who can no longer make it on his own. It is not difficult to sympathize with those homosexuals over the age of thirty-five whose lives are less than half-lived, and who find themselves sexually and socially over the hill. Empathize with the older solitary male estranged from the one life style which has offered him some degree of satisfaction, and has now paled into a jaded obsolescence from which he can seldom recover.

A case in point is this extract from an open letter published in *Gay Sunshine*, a San Francisco periodical:

"I am forty-two years old. No, no—don't tell me it doesn't matter! It does, and you know it does. . . . You know as well as I that the gay culture is youth oriented. Young guys go for young guys; and old guys go for young guys; and nobody goes for old guys. They don't even go for each other. What is the gay culture currently offering the middleaged man? Voyeurism in the clubs? A twenty-buck hustler? Fawning sycophancy as a bar-fly auntie? No thanks! . . . Isn't it ironic to go around carrying placards and giving speeches declaring, 'I'm liberated, gay and proud of it!' and to go home and go to bed alone again? . . . It's just that I have been disappointed too often to continue, especially at my age, to hope that I will find what I have been searching for so long."

## Are There Options?

Having explored the homosexual "alternative" at some length, at least a tentative evaluation is called for. In discussing the homosexual issue, let us forsake the terms "sick" and "neurotic," since they are generally misunderstood and have acquired such a pejorative connotation in our culture that their use renders a rational consideration of homosexuality impossible. Our legal processes, which bizarrely adopt a punitive approach toward the homosexual, only add fuel to irrational fires.

Homosexuality is something other than a conscious and chosen preference, or "alternative." Despite the adjurations of some members of homosexual and women's liberation groups, the homosexual is "different" in his psychological and perhaps biological orientation to the two sexes. This "difference" appears to be established long before conscious and volitional choices can rationally be evaluated. The fear of, or aversion to, the genitals of the opposite sex so frequently found in homosexuals; the compulsive aspect of their sexual behavior; the focus on the penis rather than the person; and other quantitatively greater deviations in behavior suggest a deeper and more pervasive patterning than would be explained by the "normal variance" thesis. Homosexuality appears to be an interpatterning of several biological and psychological processes which we are just beginning to dimly understand. If a prenatal endocrinal malfunction plays a major role, the environmental contribution may be only minimal. If the biological contribution is negligible or nonexistent, the "family affair" might be the dominant factor. There remain undiscovered biologic, physiologic, socio-cultural, and psychodynamic factors which await further elucidation and amplification. Obviously, I place great stress on the psychodynamic factors, for even in those whose childhood predilections indicate a predisposition toward homosexuality, parental guidance and therapy have obviated a homosexual adaptation. A prenatal hormonal "accident," if such an event is involved, can be obliterated, or at least partially erased, by a heterosexually-oriented and supportive family environment. But it may again be proven that second thoughts are ever wiser in this probably multidetermined phenomenon.

Assuming the "maladaptive" explanation for homosexuality, the question arises: Can the homosexual be made heterosexual, assuming that he wants and seeks help? The answer is a qualified but hopeful "yes," for we have statistical evidence to that effect, utilizing a psychoanalytically-oriented procedure.

Prevention is always the most efficacious treatment. Since a child's chances for happiness are greater if he is heterosexual (practically all the male and female homosexuals I have spoken to would prefer that their children be heterosexual), it is incumbent upon parents, teachers, and family physicians to become cognizant of a developing homosexual orientation so that preventative or remedial action can be taken. A father can be helped with his hostility and distantness, and a mother can be made aware of her latent seductiveness, possessiveness, and close-binding activities toward her son. Sometimes, indeed, little things mean a lot.

Most studies indicate that male and female homosexuals who enter, and remain in, psychoanalytic treatment have a 30 to 50 percent chance of making a successful heterosexual adaptation. Considering the difficulties and heartache attendant to the homosexual way of life, no opportunity should be eschewed, no rationalization should be encouraged, when the more opportune heterosexual adaptation can be obtained. The myth of the untreatability of the homosexual should be laid to rest. A study of 106 male homosexuals in psychoanalytic treatment indicated a preliminary 30 percent conversion to heterosexuality, and a five-year follow-up suggested a conversion ratio approximating 50 percent. A study of twenty-four lesbians in psychoanalysis indicated an approximate 50 percent shift toward the heterosexual end of the spectrum. Other studies show similar results. I would hope that these reports disprove the assertion that "No homosexual has ever been successfully treated by psychoanalysis," but I doubt that they will.

Assuming that homosexuality is often amenable to change, we are left with the question of who should seek treatment. There is no point in insisting that a man happy with, and committed to, a homosexual adaptation attempt to change it. Happiness is a rare commodity in a shaky and dissatisfied world, and if someone has found the key that fits comfortably for him, he should ardently clutch it and make it work for him as best he can. There is no reason to doubt that some homosexuals with long-standing relationships have found precisely that. There are three primary reasons, however, for a homosexually-oriented man or woman to enter psychiatric treatment:

1. Unhappiness and dissatisfaction with homosexuality as a way of life
2. The appearance of symptom formation, anxiety, depression, suicidal thoughts, alcoholism, and the myriad of other evidences of distress which impel others, heterosexual or homosexual, to seek psychiatric assistance
3. Identity confusion, primarily found in the teen years and early twenties, in which the male has conflicting heterosexual and homosexual pulls and desires, and has still to delineate himself as an adult male in his particular society.

A primary indication of the desirability of psychiatric intervention is the onset of the more conventional symptomatology expressive of conflictual situations which the man can no longer handle effectively. Attacks of acute anxiety, with "heart palpitations," restlessness, insomnia, and recurring nightmares, are signals of distress. Depressions, characterized by overwhelming feelings of sadness and despondency, ideas of worthlessness, and self-abnegation, with either a restless agitation or a marked diminution of activity, may eventuate in recurring suicidal thoughts and possibly suicidal attempts. These evidences of psychological stress plague both heterosexuals and homosexuals, and call for psychiatric intervention in either group. The homosexual life itself may be an important causative factor in some men. In certain men, it may be necessary that a heterosexual adaptation be attempted, while others can best be assisted to more successfully adapt to their homosexuality. The argument advanced by some homosexual groups, to wit: "The symptoms you delineate, dear doctor, stem from society's oppression of the homosexual, and are not intrinsic to the homosexual himself," has some truth to it. Most certainly, the attitude of our cultural institutions has frequently been oppressive and dehumanizing, and sometimes brutal. But of what avail is this argument to the particular man, saturated with more symptoms than he can handle, scratching about in a world he never created? It may be good propaganda, but it is poor treatment.

Identity confusion is found among those whose sexual identities have been insufficiently defined, whose life experiences have contributed little to a sense of self, or of confidence and assurance as functional males in their society. Their assessment of the male role is often monstrously distorted and exaggerated, while their own capacities are pitifully underrated. Expectations of chronic ineffectuality readily seep into the sexual areas of their lives. Fearful and insecure, and beset by doubts of their masculine adequacy, they flee from the crucible of the heterosexual confrontation into a homosexual haven. The opportunity to seek gratification for dependency and power yearnings, to escape from the label of a human "failure" into a new identity exotically "different," encourages the vulnerable heterosexual to submerge himself in the homosexual subculture—an actor in a tenuously constructed play who is miscast in the part.

My strongest objection to the militantly homosexual groups who advocate "Hey, hey, hey, try it once the other way," is that by strongly advocating and proselytizing homosexuality as "normal" or a preferable alternative to heterosexuality, they discourage the inchoate male who can be substantially helped with his sexual identity problems from taking that basic step: the recognition and admission of his difficulty, coupled with a determination

to do something constructive about it. One can understand and empathize with a minority group, rudely
pushed to the fringes of society, seeking self-justification,
respectability, and an equal share in whatever remains of
common humanity. The secure heterosexual is neither
threatened nor disturbed by homosexual advocacy, while
the confirmed homosexual may derive helpful reinforcement and comfort from it. But, as usual, it is the insecure
and vulnerable who pay the price, and the payment is
extended over a lifetime.

When the chanting is stilled and the placards stored
away, when the homosexual is liberated and all men are
regarded as equal brethren, I suspect that the final words
will be Merle Miller's, written with much poignancy
about his own homosexuality: "Gay is good. Gay is proud.
Well, yes, I suppose. If I had been given a choice (but
who is), I would prefer to have been straight."

# 6

# Hot Cockles and Husbands

## *"Hot Cockles"*

"HOT COCKLES" is a sixteenth-century English country game in which a blindfolded player tries to guess who hit him. It is currently being resurrected on a more sophisticated and psychic plane, with a significant crop of contemporary husbands serving as the befuddled man in the middle. Pelted from all sides by invidious insults, he neither comprehends what is happening to him nor knows where the next blow will originate. Suddenly men are hearing the more fractious of the feminist set proclaim "Marriage is Hell," and many husbands who had assumed a lifetime of indescribable bliss now find themselves portrayed as Satans overseeing their daemonic domains. Patriarchy is deemed paganism, housewifery is equated with slavery, and motherhood is pictured as some monstrous miasma into which the female has been forced by her surly spermatic spouse.

Unaware that covert but nonetheless compelling forces are set on changing the rules of the marital game, these husbands have blithely believed that what was good enough for their fathers was good enough for them. And why not? They were trained for it from infancy, and their Oedipus Complexes were resolved by the determination to find a girl just like the girl who married dear old Dad. Somnambulating in their Provider robes and anchored to their Achiever Complexes, they seemed justified in their belief that women never had it so good. A recent Gallup poll indicating that the majority of women questioned felt they lead more pleasant lives than men provided a statistical seal of approval to this assumption. "Marriage," they are now informed, "is terrible, and husbands have made it so." Hot Cockles!

Marriage is a universal social institution designed to provide a congenial milieu for the maximal well-being of the individual, while insuring the maximal stability of his social order. It is a functional arrangement which offers an effective economic utilization and consumption of products, an assured sex life, and a manageable method for the generation, legitimation, and rearing of offspring. Benjamin Franklin noted its practical utility in his "Advice on the Choice of a Mistress": "It is the man and woman united that makes the complete human being. Separate, she wants his force of body and strength of reason; he, her softness, sensibility, and acute discernment. Together, they are more likely to succeed in the world. A single man has not nearly the value he would have in a state of union. He is an incomplete animal, he resembles the odd half of a pair of scissors. If you get a prudent, healthy wife, your industry in your profession, with her good economy, will be a fortune sufficient."

Aristotle viewed marriage and family as "an association established by nature for the supply of everyday wants." One might add that marriage also allows the fulfillment of a basic human need which individuals cannot fulfill by themselves: an ongoing intimate relationship with another person. It has always served as the vehicle for the satisfaction of a host of unconscious needs as well, such as dependency, security, and self-esteem. In an increasingly impersonal society, there is a necessity for personal warmth and intimate relatedness. Marriage and family have been the traditional bastion, the refuge of the individual from the neutrality or downright hostility of the world outside the home. Although an admittedly imperfect instrument, marriage has remained the most rational physical, emotional, and pragmatic arrangement for most people in the ordering of their lives.

But the past decade has witnessed a wholesale onslaught against marital and family institutions. Marriage is currently being compared to a besieged fortress, with those outside the walls trying to get in, while the defenders inside desperately pray to escape unscathed. Of course occasional sorties against home and hearth are not new. Kate Millett's prediction that marriage will wither away and Ms. Greer's carefree counsel to women to remain single are tepid puffs compared to August Strindberg's: "The Family! Home of all social evils, a charitable institution for indolent women, a prison workshop for the slaving breadwinner, and a hell for children." These words were written more than a hundred years ago, yet the marriage rate has continued to rise. But the frequency, the popularity, and the social acceptability of these attacks have increased astronomically. A Ms. Balogun suggests that the personal relationships of marriage must undergo a revolution. Her suggestion is the eventual dissolution of marriage, with the establishment of all-female communes in its place. Her sagacity is exceeded only by the viability of her alternative. Ms. Linda Gordon proclaims: "The nuclear family must be destroyed, and people must find better ways of living together." What better ways, given the complex society in which we live? Further mention of similar antimarriage critiques could go on ad infinitum, and sometimes do ad nauseum, but the themes are repetitive, the solutions a tribute to obfuscation, and the Husband inevitably labeled "It" in this latest and perhaps most serious round of Hot Cockles.

Nuptial blessedness is evidently suffering from an acute case of manic-depression, complicated by a touch of sheer hysteria. From the manic perspective, marriage is more popular in the United States than at any other time in history. In 1971, more than two-thirds of all Americans above the age of fourteen were married. Compare this with the year 1890, the first year of reasonably accurate statistical reportage, in which 56.6 percent of women and 53.9 percent of men were married. The bull market in bridegrooms has steadily risen for the past eighty years, and shows no signs of abating. Indeed, the marriage rate has skyrocketed 26 percent in the past ten years. In 1972, the number of males opting to become husbands had increased by 73,000 over the previous year, to the impressive total of 2,269,000! Apparently marriage as an institution is not moribund. The citizenry appears to be breaking down the doors of neighborhood churches, synagogues, and city halls in a frantic surge of knot-tying.

Unfortunately, many of the knots, poorly made, unravel rather speedily. The symptomatology of marriage's depressed phase is highlighted by the 70,000 per month, or 3,333 per day, which are being dissolved through divorce or annulment. More than four in ten marital unions go on the rocks, after a mean life of 6.9 years, and divorce has increased by 80 percent compared to ten years ago. Sixteen million divorced men and women wander these United States. While the vast majority remarry, the urge to take the plunge a second time appears to be abating. Two-thirds of divorces involve children, and one child in every six has divorced parents. These children's chances of becoming involved in divorce themselves are significantly higher than the norm. The somewhat dismal data have been interpreted as an invitation to hysterical imprecation by the connubial Cassandras. Midst the screeching, it is understandable that many harassed husbands, feeling hustled and hot-cockled, wonder how it all came about.

## The Blindfold

The motive forces behind marriage have ranged from the pragmatic to the romantic, from survival to "love." In simpler times, up to a century or two ago, the pragmatic was clearly and admittedly predominant. The complementarity of male and female roles added to the survival of each. The pioneering husband busted the sod and built the cabin, while his wife baked the bread and basted the buckskin. After an Eskimo bridegroom returned with his catch of caribou meat, his bride would chew his boots to prevent them from freezing and cracking. This enabled the man to hunt again the next day. The Irish farmer, rooted to the soil, married only "when the land needed a woman." Since this need only arose when his mother could no longer perform her household chores, the average age of the rural Irish bridegroom hovered around thirty-eight. The land and its requirements were paramount, affection or romance were laughable inconsequentials.

An extension of the survival motif was the derivation of physical and/or economic comfort from marriage. In 1596, Shakespeare wrote: "I come to wive it wealthily in Padua/ If wealthily then happily in Padua." Three hundred and fifty-two years later, in 1948, Broadway audiences convulsed with appreciative laughter when Cole Porter, appropriating this refreshing candor in *Kiss Me*,

*Kate*, added: "If my wife has a bag of gold/ Do I care if the bag be old?/ I've come to wive it wealthily in Padua."[*]
Perhaps times have not changed too much. This quintessential quid pro quo, this "you scratch my back and I'll scratch yours," unquestionably resulted in many workable, albeit businesslike marriages. Since prolonged proximity has been known to produce a passionate intimacy, many must have been hotly successful.

The survival functions also expanded to include the welfare of the individual's family, relatives, or tribe. In these instances, the prospective spouses served as agents for their group, contracting economic, proprietary, and social alliances. While these contracts were primarily for the benefit of their kith and kin, the contractor partook of the multitude of benefits afforded by his group. The arranged marriages may have had a paucity of passion, but ensconcement within an extended family and a certain surety of permanence were not altogether unreasonable tradeoffs. If love developed subsequently, so much the better. Stars may not have veered from their orbits, emotional skyrockets may not have exploded, but marriage held firm, producing generation after generation. Matters might have been worse.

The rise of the Romantic began in the nineteenth century, more distinctly in the Anglo-Saxon world, and most pronouncedly in the United States. By this time, the more primitive survival problems had either been dealt with already or the responsibility for their solution had passed from the family domicile to the more dubious domain of society. Society implicitly pledged to a man the physical safety of himself and his family, the education of his children, the enrichment of his retirement years, and, in a burst of paternalistic enthusiasm, offered life, liberty, and the pursuit of happiness. The functions of the family became shared by legislators, jurists, and a presumably benevolent bureaucracy.

The breakdown of the extended family (several related generations functioning as a single household and/or economic unit) was accelerated by the Industrial Revolution. Urban anonymity produced alienated souls shuttling between masses of people and isolated apartments.

In the evolution of marriage, the struggle for physical existence gave way to the scramble for emotional sustenance and psychic survival. A man sought his roots in the establishment of his own nuclear family (father, mother, and children). Marriage became transformed into a stronghold of affection, security, and a sense of permanency; a refuge from loneliness in which a man could let his guard down and still find contentment in an uncaring or inimical universe; a redoubt in which he could feel important to, and share an intimacy with, another fellow human; a milieu to develop within, a springboard for emotional growth after the storms of adolescence. With an assured sexual relationship serving as the *pièce de résistance*, affectionate marriage became a highly marketable commodity. It filled a need, had no competition, and seemed reasonably priced. Future customers were trained in and for it since childhood, and knew that they faced social disapprobation should they abstain from the sale. An idea whose time had most assuredly arrived. The affectionate ideal cornered the matrimonial market. The practical had ceded to the romantic, hearts palpitated a wee bit faster, and lovers could be observed scattering into the sunsets and other similarly blinding scenes.

But modern civilization has developed a mania for merchandising. The marketing gimmick of the affectionate relationship became "love." "Love and marriage" became as conjoined as the horse and carriage. "True love" was romanticized and sanctified in magazines, books, movies, and in all other communications media, invoked as a *deus ex machina* when things got a bit tough. Evidently when love was here to stay, bills would get paid, interpersonal conflicts resolved, and, in making love, not war, mankind seemed headed for a Second Coming which would grant a renegotiated lease on the Garden of Eden. Love became the *raison d'être* of marriage, and vice versa. The more mundane factors such as similar value systems, socio-economic backgrounds, compatible levels of aspiration, and mutual respect took subsidiary roles to such adolescent jabberings as: "But we love each other; what more do we need?" The answer, in all likelihood, could be a good divorce lawyer.

A French proverb cautions: "Try to reason about love, and you will lose your reason." Any such discussion is considered sacrilegious. While a "Prisoner of Love" may sell more than a million records, a critic of love runs the risk of being vituperatively branded a misanthrope. Analyzing love, one is told, is like dissecting a frog to learn how it functions. You may expose the component organs, but in the end you are left with a dead frog. However, men have not only married and sacrificed for love, they have also died in its name.

"Love" is a four-letter word which covers so much territory while defining so little that it has become all but devoid of semantic utility. While it may be the touchstone of the poet and the philosopher, it can be a psychiatrist's unending labyrinth. The Hanunoo of the Philippine Islands, a rice-growing culture, have ninety-two words for "rice." Their stomachs and their economy depend on knowing precisely what they are talking about. Eskimos use eleven words for "snow." Its varied forms and textures have a life-and-death significance for them. Yet we have but one word for "love." I love my wife, and I love my children. I also love Peking duck, scuba diving, and the Marx Brothers. Love, it seems, has a ghostly quality. Everyone talks about it, but no one can pin it down. Voltaire agrees with me, which is always refreshing. "Love has various lodgings," he noted; "the same word does not always signify the same thing."

"Love" can be used in contradictory contexts by the same person. "Love is, after all, the gift of oneself," says Jean Anouilh. In another play, he exactly contradicts his previous definition, stating: "I think the only reason one loves, *monsieur*, is for his own pleasure." It may have different meanings at different stages of one's life. John Ciardi observed that "Love is the word used to label the sexual excitement of the young, the habituation of the middle-aged, and the mutual dependency of the old."

Still, if "what the world needs now is love, sweet love," and since man will evidently persist in mouthing that which he cannot define, perhaps the following is at least a working concept: Love is a caring extension of one's psychological boundaries to incorporate another human being as a part of oneself. It involves the establishment of an ongoing mutual identity. It overcomes the divisiveness, alienation, and separateness which underlie the human condition, and provides a partner for the building and development of a chain of life experiences. Love is to be distinguished from passions more limited in scope, such as affection, infatuation, and sexual romance. "Affection" is a "caring for" or warmth felt toward another person. It does not, however, involve the incorporation of the object of affection into one's psychological self. "Infatuation" is a transient albeit ecstatic reaction to an idealized image of the partner. "I met this perfectly wonderful girl in this perfectly marvelous place . . ." is a case in point. "Sexual romance" is the gilding of the glandular with an aura of the profound, another instance of relational sex being invoked to ennoble a genital excursion. When Robert Graves defined love as "a universal migraine/ a bright stain on the vision/ Blotting out reason," I think he was really defining sexual passion.

It appears that love has become an oversold and misunderstood element in marriage. Alone, it is insufficient; misinterpreted, it produces disappointment and disillusion. Unaccompanied by the cement of similar socio-economic backgrounds, value structures, and life goals, marriage for "love" is a fragile entity, with the bridegroom having unwittingly purchased a ticket to a game of Hot Cockles.

## The Players

It may be a blessing that most men marry for reasons of which they are essentially unaware. Romantic rationalizations to the contrary, marriages are arranged, not in Heaven, but in the unconscious psyches of the participants. A man's unexplained intuitive feel is frequently more perceptive than his rationality. Thus, with all the women in the world to choose from, the average man marries a girl who lives within a half-mile radius of his parental home. The fact that he is most likely to meet a girl who patronizes the same supermarket, church, or tavern is only a partial factor. The neighborhood girl is more apt to share his social, economic, and cultural background, as well as his expectations of marriage. Since she will probably come from similar ethnic stock, she will also remind him more of his mother than would a strange girl from a strange city. The color of her hair and eyes, her figure, her voice with its inflections, are prone to call up associations with the women of his childhood, with their associated warmth and security. This feeling of familiarity, this meshing of similarities and complementarities, are major determinants in the mating game, and are probably most conducive to marital stability.

Few, if any, marriages are devoid of their unconscious deals and fantasies, with their evocation of power, dependency, and other strivings which were implanted from infancy onward. Some men unknowingly marry to create a private empire to rule, in sharp contrast to the relative impotency they may have experienced as a child or as an adult operating in the outside world. An only child, accustomed to being the sun about whom the planets revolve, may bring a similar expectation into marriage. An oldest child, with his predilection for performance may assume a somber, caretaking role in wedlock, and a youngest son might envision marriage as a game in which he is nurtured and applauded. Should wifely responses to any of these types of men be other than compliance, awe, passivity, or approval, watch out for Hot Cockles. The variations are manifold, but since the game is played on an unconscious level, our player is generally blindfolded and unknowing.

It may be of solace to the cockled gamesman to appreciate the fact that women are subject to the same unconscious drives, invested with their own set of rules. Fortunately, people tend to zero in on those whose personalities and needs best nestle with their own. More marriages still survive than fall apart.

## The Changing Game

The marital game plan has never been rigid or static. As society evolved, the form of marriage evolved with it, continually adapting to the latest social reality. From economic cooperation to romantic union, marriage adjusted, much as baseball has to the designated hitter, or football to the two-platoon system. The game remained the same, although its complexion has been somewhat modified. But the tempo of social change has exploded within the past quarter of a century, and the homeostasis of the marital and the familial has been swamped by changes too vast and too rapid to be readily assimilated. Simultaneously pelted by a fusillade of problems, contemporary marriage has had to juggle a technologic tyranny with its attendant Era of Impermanence; the breakup of the extended family, with the loss of a network of clan support; the ensuing overload of pressures upon the nuclear family to fill the gaps; increased isolation within the family units themselves; attacks on marriage and parenthood; and the promulgation of more radical marriage forms in place of the conventional, to mention a few. That marriage has continued to weather the storm as well as it has is a tribute to its basic underlying strengths.

It would be foolhardy, however, not to recognize that the state of the marital union has become somewhat unstable. Familial ties have loosened, and more and more family jewels are on display in pawnshop windows. The Industrial Revolution scattered family members from the old homesteads to varied cities throughout the nation, and the movement continues. One-quarter of the population changes residence each year, uprooting any small tendrils that might have begun to sprout. Since our new technology requires the continuous production and consumption of new models to keep our friendly assembly line going, the theme of transiency, of impermanency, is programmed into our psyches. If cars, plastic dishes, and paper napkins are made to be used and quickly discarded, why not project this onto human relationships? Friendships and acquaintances come and go at a dizzying pace, children leave the nest before they have even learned to fly, and divorce insurance is applied for as soon as the "I do's" are murmured. Since marriage deals with some ideal of permanency, it is rapidly being placed at a competitive disadvantage compared with proponents of the ideal of change for the sake of change. Our brave new culture has also created the commuting father, a phantasmal transient, whose occupation and role are often a mystery to both his children and his wife. It has impaired a son's identification with his father, increasing the probability of excessive dependency and delinquency in the boy, and deprived the putative patriarch of the enjoyment of his children. The traditional family dinner, where the various members dined together, exchanging ideas and experiences, has gone the way of the Toonerville Trolley. This mutual conclave has been replaced by the T.V. dinner, eaten haphazardly and in solitude, in front of television sets portraying caricatured family situations in which parents are hare-brained half-wits and children are the repository of wisdom. Fathers, in particular, are presented as lovable boobs and hapless innocents who are extricated from ludicrous gaffes by their frequently silly but worldly-wise wives. A laudable example to present to children each evening. Parents and their children become increasingly estranged from each other, and the schism between all generations widens. Amid those islands of isolation, grandparents find themselves divorced from functional utility, except for occasional baby-sitting, and eventually emigrate to Florida or other "retirement villages" to await death in the sunshine.

This indelicate shredding of the social fabric has both contributed to and highlighted what may prove to be the most critical issue of our time: the validity and continuance of intrahuman bonding and the future form of all emotional linkages. Is the lasting emotional bond passé, dysfunctional and anachronistic, or should men fight like hell to keep and to strengthen it? Are permanent male-female relationships the "closed-dyad disease" indulged in "only by crazy people," or are they the only alternative to a lifelong sequence of passing bumps, a series of inconsequential caroms from one person to another, relatively devoid of significance? Has humanity finally progressed from the Age of the Home to the Millennium of the Motel? If this is so, what are the consequences? Since the nuclear family is the ultimate in permanent bonding, it has become targeted as the focal point of the controversy.

With forty-seven million husbands standing by as interested but confused spectators, the trial of the American family is being reported on in every major magazine and newspaper in the land. It has become the subject of television serials, in which ravaged units are presented as "An American Family."

The case against the family portrays a harassed husband tied by legal thongs to his bored and infantilized spouse, a sorry being who has sacrificed her claim to personhood to the stereotyped mediocrity of child rearing and homemaking, a candidate for depression when the nest has become emptied of its fledglings. Locked into an unnatural monogamy, a statistical freak in the history of humankind's arrangements, the two turn inward, wrenching a semblance of support from each other under the guise of a legislated and sanctified togetherness. This closed unit acts as fertile soil for the germination of jealousy and possessiveness, in which privacy, separateness, and extrafamilial emotional contacts are looked upon as disruptive and disloyal. The children of this happy union are portrayed as hapless victims of oppression and domination by parents who visit their own neuroses on their progeny, thereby generating and further perpetuating humanity's slide into a neurotic netherworld.

"Motherhood" and "fatherhood" might be regarded as epithets describing society's unenlightened sheep. After all, if "Marriage is Hell," it follows that "Mother's Day is over." The typical antimaternal complaint bemoans the woeful effects that kiddies have on sex and marriage, the restrictions placed upon the mother's freedom, and the wearisome fatigue involved in child rearing, with its ennui, its anxieties, and the wretched inconvenience of it all. Apparently in our plasticized wonderland, no one is to be inconvenienced. Boredom and fatigue are either to be eliminated from our vocabulary or become neatly encapsulated within the wonderful workaday world of men. In like fashion, "fatherhood" is surely the greatest folly since Seward's. Since fathers see less of their children, who cost more to raise and provide greater headaches along with fewer satisfactions, the male opting for fatherhood must be either insane or inane.

Defenders of the family, if they possess a minimum of honesty and good sense, admit to the partial validity of these charges, although they may detect a hint of the caricature in them. The defender's ultimate response is a "Yes, but . . . what is the alternative?" Civilization, to survive, must be pragmatic, and, as yet, no alternative systems less imperfect than the family have been offered. The basic human needs, security, commitment, intimacy, interdependency, and the humanizing effects of child rearing, are seldom to be found outside the permanent bonds of the family. How many men can claim they have reaped these benefits from a series of revolving-door relationships? Admittedly, monogamy is an artificial device fostered by society to insure its stability. But even among the more gonadally driven men I have treated, after a while faces blur, one crotch begins to resemble another, and the gyrations of last week's partner become indistinguishable from tonight's, and the majority eventually reach a point where they would happily trade the fling for the familiar, the chimera of the chase for the actuality of devotion.

A stable civilization requires a stable citizenry, and vice versa. The universal parental function has been the preparation of offspring to survive as independent adults. This preparation occurs best in what Heinz Hartmann referred to as the "average expectable environment," a milieu characterized by reasonable limits, expectations, and predictable responses from the important people in a child's environment. If he did A, he could count on receiving B. If he was helpful, for example, he could expect praise, while if he was disruptive, he would expect and receive a reprimand. If the environment becomes unpredictable, anxiety and instability eventuate. In this admittedly ideal family setting, a child develops a sense of security and rationality which he will subsequently convey to his society. Where can this environment be better assembled than in the family? Sequential parents, one-parent families, or parents abandoning their roles as parents to schools, peer groups, and the like will not suffice. We would face generations of children who grow as weeds, untended, uncared for, and uncultivated, devoid of any standards by which to orient themselves. Granted, parenting has become progressively difficult. With the current societal tumult, a father frequently finds himself bewildered, not only as to what the future environment will be for his offspring, but also as to the current norms. What does a father tell his daughter, for example, about premarital virginity? His gut reaction might be to say, "Keep it, hold onto it," but is this really to her benefit? Might not premarital sexual experience actually aid her marriage? Many authorities think so. How honest, forthright, and assertive should he advise his son to be in the vocational rat race? Should he promote or discourage aggressive behavior in his progeny, when their society is becoming increasingly predatory and violent? In the past, the answers to the aforementioned questions seemed pat, standard, and constant. But sure responses to these and hundreds of other questions have been shattered, and it is only the courageous, interested, and loving parent who will come to grips with them, earn the respect and affection of his children, and exact the joys of parenting, which have become so chic to deride. When speaking of fathers, let's stop talking of Archie Bunkers and Dagwood Bumsteads, and talk of heroes instead.

Amid the welter of pros and cons, the impression sticks that the discovery of the nuclear family is one of those happy accidents which occasionally befall the human race. In tampering with such a universal institution, a critic or social reformer should be cautious, lest in fixing upon an item, he loses the entire agenda. Obliterate the family, with nothing more substantative in its stead, and you will produce a different type of human being: a non-relating, amoral, emotionally and intellectually crippled soul, an angry entity who is capable of raising the temperature of social turmoil to levels incompatible with the survival of civilization as we know it.

In the midst of the deluge stands the husband, lately profaned and defamed. He has already made his investment, based on good faith and upon centuries of human experience, but the bottom appears to be dropping out. Has he been foolish or farsighted, coerced or courageous? The answer will not be known until the current home stand of Hot Cockles is played out.

## Pitfalls and Penalties

Hot Cockles reaches its peak intensity during divorce, with the courtroom serving as an oak-paneled arena. At the docket stand the eight to nine hundred thousand husbands who are divorced each year, with an equivalent number loosening up in the bullpen, taking the pre-scribed and ritualized steps preparatory to their day in Splitsville. Facing the presiding judge, the average divorc-ing male is prone to hallucinate. He imagines a black-robed avenging angel, sternly preparing an emotional and financial guillotine, for when the legal machinations have run their course, the cockled gamesman will feel himself severed from his heart and his wallet. Frequently, he will not understand why.

A column in *The New York Times* entitled "I Am One Man, Hurt," tragically underlines the dismal point. Writ-ing under a pseudonym, the author informs us that he is in the process of being divorced, but "I don't want to be, I am horrified by the prospect, I think it is the most devastating thing that could happen to my family, but it is going to take place. My wife wants it." How did it come to pass? "I thought we were a perfectly happy family until my wife told me, without any advance warn-ing, that she didn't love me anymore and wanted a divorce. Not a matter of infidelity or alcoholism or beat-ing or arguments or desertion, but that it didn't mean anything to her anymore and she wanted out." The author's understandable agony, an increasing common-place, ends with the despairing cry of the archetypal protagonist of Hot Cockles: "I am one man, hurt, groping. I do not have answers to the most important questions of my life. But I think that for the good of all of us, as a people and as a society, we had better start coming up with better ones than we have now." Amen.

Unless the divorced man has his next inamorata waiting in the courthouse corridor, he will likely emerge somewhat stunned, feeling alone in the world of the singles, torn by feelings of guilt, failure, and anger. The mystical oneness is split in twain, the partnership is now a solo enterprise, and his other self has become an alien and perhaps avaricious entity. Estrangement from his children, that most unacceptable of nightmares, becomes progressively more vivid, until the first visitation weekend, when the bad dream becomes a stomach-crunching reality. Inexorably, the "high cost of leaving" seeps its way into his consciousness. If he is childless, alimony will devour only one-quarter to one-third of his income; but if he is among the two-thirds of divorcing males who boast of fatherhood, he will astonishingly observe one-third to one-half of his after-tax income evaporating in alimony and child support, horrendously excoriating his meager standard of living and labeling him a financial cripple to any of the female sex who might consider him a reasonable risk for a subsequent matrimonial adventure. After the legal fees, child support, division of property, and adagios with the Internal Revenue Service, the severing male conceives of himself as an economic eunuch, normal in appearance, but functionally sterile.

His erstwhile spouse, now socially saddled by her children, financially fettered, and facing a lonely and uncertain future, understandably feels sorely used and embittered. Should she reenter the dating rat race, she perceives herself as dehumanized, fair game for philandering husbands and just another aging slab on a neverending meat rack. Her antagonism toward her ex escalates, and the friendliest and most civil of divorces tend to sour. Some divorcées devote the remainder of their lives to a vendetta against their onetime love, choosing vengeance over sanity, and often wreck both lives in the process. Previous comfortings are replaced by mutual cruelties, and the embattled participants become too pre-occupied to understand.

When the legal lacerations have stopped bleeding, the cockled combatant might reflect on the hows and whys of the wreckage, conducting a psychological post mortem upon the corpse. People seldom divorce with the conscious awareness of precisely what went wrong. They dissolve out of desperation and disappointment, out of a concatenation of feelings which, having been left unat-tended to fester, finally seemed to cry out for separation rather than repair and reconciliation.

The divorces of the past were more cut and dried, and readily identifiable in their causation. Callous cruelty, drunkenness, desertion, and uncontrolled lechery were sufficient and understandable. The divorce proceedings resembled morality plays in which evil was confronted by good, was adjudged at fault, and received its just and proper punishment. But in these less moralistic times, no-fault divorce has arrived, and rightfully so. While those baser and more blatant justifications still exist for uncoupling, psychiatrists and lawyers are increasingly seeing divorce situations stemming from a new discord-ancy, in which a previously stable and fairly harmonious equilibrium had somehow grown dissonant. Rather than searching for the villain of the piece, more attention is being paid to the patterns of the interpersonal relation-ships within a marriage. More attempts are being made to ascertain the sources of the splitting, to rectify them if possible, or to at least prevent their repetition the next time around.

Upsurgences of discordancy have both intrapsychic and circumstantial origins. The former would include the psychological patterns and problems of the participants, the fantasies versus the actualities of their marriage, and the congruity of their meshing; while the latter encompasses the sociologic milieu and the extrinsic unforeseen circumstances which may impinge on the best of complex and long-standing relationships.

From the sociological vantage point, the odds seem stacked against youth and brevity. The teen-age marriage, for example, with its ignorance and inexperience, brief courtship and engagement, lacking an adequate trial of compatibility and togetherness, produces a high quota of disentanglements. An urban environment and low socio-economic status inject an added note of instability which statistically increases the probability of divorce. Dissimilar backgrounds and mixed marriages lack the communality required for mutuality.

The exigencies of life have their unsettling effects. Financial incapabilities and reverses, in-law problems, the birth of children with significant mental or physical incapacities, chronic illness, and the like can add a sufficiently high stress factor to crumble a reasonably well-constructed home.

The intrapsychic factors, however, are finally attaining their share of the limelight, as testified to by the increased amount of space devoted to them in the popular press and magazines. All individuals have their neurotic quirks and patterns which they bring to a marriage along with their hygienic habits and table manners. Marital proximity focuses on and often accentuates these traits, either to the betterment or detriment of the relationship. The spouse who flies high wedded to a spouse whose feet are firmly fixed on earth, or the intellectual espoused to an emotional respondent, may produce very workable partnerships. Sadists and masochists make excellent mates, as do alcoholics and martyrs and machismic males and dependent females. As long as each continues in his or her prescribed role, the relationship blossoms. Should one partner change, however, through growth, fatigue, or becoming just fed up, the equilibrium is unsettled and dissolution looms.

Other matched peculiarities may not be so fortuitous, however. While optimists will invest much of themselves in a marriage, the more pessimistically inclined will close themselves off and invite separation. Paranoid traits have served as excellent catalysts for divorce. The associated excessive suspicion and distrust tend to increase after the ceremony, terminating in unanswerable charges and accusations against the innocent spouse, who, unless delighting in masochism, will eventually proffer charges of his own via a divorce attorney.

The fantasies and the actualities of marriage are seldom totally congruent. When they are sufficiently divergent, the reality is rendered unlivable, even among the best-intentioned. Some women, from puberty onward, immerse themselves in richly romanticized fantasies, from the cute "meet" through the "whirlwind courtship" to the final "I do"—and there the fantasy abruptly ends. The actualities of day-to-day living with a man contrasted with the facades utilized during dating were never seriously considered or anticipated. Tempers and toilet paper, dishes and diapers, the unappreciated gesture and the unshaven husband, come as shockingly alien concepts. Numerous women complain of sexual frigidity occurring immediately after their marriage, despite the swingingly orgastic premarital relationships they enjoyed with their husbands-to-be. Once the "illicit" play had given way to the sanctioned reality, they closed up and froze up. Early demands for separation or divorce were a surprise only to their husbands.

Similarly, a man might visualize marriage as merely

an addition of a permanent Bunny to his Playboy pad, a lithesome testament to his masculinity. After the hippety-hopping has run its course, and the plaything asserts her personhood, the questions of responsibility, relatedness, and family arise, and the pad may be perceived as a prison, an institution to escape from.

The variants are many. Among those inwardly convinced of their basic unacceptability, the "if you really love me, you'll accept me at my worst" gambit may be employed. Its practitioners unwittingly test the affections of their spouse by presenting themselves at their worst, with the delusion that, if the spouse sticks, they are somehow worthwhile. The rub is that the only spouse who would stand for this ploy is either markedly self-effacing or masochistic. In the event that the partner refuses the test, the practitioner generally hears his worst detailed from the witness box. Or consider the man with the perpetually open mouth, waiting to be fed. He fantasizes marriage as a return to the womb, with his wife serving as a primordial mother, the source of an ever-flowing cornucopia of goodies with which she is to nurture and care for him. Should she slip, should a meal be delayed or one of his directives overlooked, the man-child reverts to temper tantrums. The perpetual turbulence frequently terminates in divorce.

A major but insufficiently appreciated cause of marital disruption is the inability of one or both partners to adapt to the changes which are intrinsic to the maturation of a marriage. The typical marriage has its life cycle, with its sequence of stages, each stage evoking some degree of disequilibrium which necessitates readjustment and reintegration. The process might be compared to a steeplechase race, a zesty and challenging course with its sequence of hurdles and obstacles which must be perceived and gracefully overcome. A hurdle poorly managed or failed might permanently disqualify the contestant. He may opt out of steeplechasing forever, or try again with a new partner in another race. But it is the high hurdles of the steeplechase which capture the imagination and make or break a marriage.

The first and most hazardous hurdle is the postnuptial period. The high number of divorces occurring within the first two years of marriage is ample evidence of the difficulty of this stage. Here one confronts the fragmented prenuptial fantasies, the obviously erroneous mismatches, the too-hasty elopements, and the pathos of the person basically unsuited to marriage. When one uses marriage to escape from the family homestead, the patterns of the past obtrude upon the present, unwanted and unwittingly, to the escapee's dissatisfaction and the spouse's consternation. It is by no means an easy jump, yet most make it and progress to the second, some two or three years away.

The second hurdle is reached with the birth of the first child, when the "couple" becomes the "family." The seven pounds of squalling protoplasm concretizes the marital commitment and adds a new quota of contentments and complexities to the life of the couple. The husband must now accept ceding the center of the stage to the newcomer, and the wife must feel sufficiently competent to nurture, or have the means to find sufficient help to adequately do the job. In the era of the extended family, there was generally a sufficiency of helpers to assist the fledgling mother, but in the more isolated nuclear family of today, this assistance is frequently absent and the maternal tenderfoot may feel chained to the bassinet and the sandbox, unappreciated by her husband. Furthermore, the couple must combat the jealousies, possessiveness, and resurgences of ancient sibling rivalries which the child evokes. Insecure mothers may resent a child's positive responses to his father as evidence of their own maternal inadequacy. The births of subsequent children bring additional pleasures and stresses, necessitating further adaptations within the family constellation. In one instance, a father who as an oldest child had resented the birth of his younger brothers strongly identified with his first child and rejected his subsequent children. The consequent battles with his wife, with the drawing up of sides within the family unit, all but dissolved the family until the issues were exposed and clarified via his psychoanalytic exploration.

The third obstacle, somewhat smaller and less treacherous than the first two, has lately been popularized and perhaps heightened by the efforts and writing of the feminologists. The hurdle coincides with the entry of the last child into school. No longer primarily preoccupied with child care, the wife, now in her mid-thirties, looks forward to the remaining forty years and wonders what they will be like. She has read articles and listened to lecturers inform her that worthwhileness and individuality stem from productivity outside the home, and that she unwisely sacrificed her personhood for her family. Perhaps it is not too late to rejoin the rest of humanity in its march to achieve. But her family functioning has left her vocationally crippled, or at least retarded, and now, no longer able to rely on infant rearing as the *raison d'être* of her existence, she may feel somewhat befuddled and lost and look to her husband for support and reassurance. He, however, is having problems of his own. He is now in his late thirties, approaching the fitful forties, the make-or-break years of his career. It is the beginning of his final push for position, and the call of his corporation frequently is heard above the distress of his wife and the cries of his children. Feeling adrift, more wives are turning to alcohol or extramarital affairs at this point, for that final fling before menopause.

The fourth hurdle is reached when the youngest child finally leaves home and enters the world outside, creating the now infamous "empty nest." The child-centeredness of the couple's past twenty years is now only a collection of memories and old photographs, and the original pair is once again a twosome. But the couple has changed, jointly and individually. While a renaissance of the dyad must be devised, the obstacles are considerable. The husband is now in his late forties or early fifties, and may acutely feel himself closer to the end than to the beginning. His life's ambitions and aspirations are perceived as unrealized and he must come to terms with this fact of his life. Having probably experienced an occasional episode of sexual inadequacy, he may feel his prowess waning and search for an extramarital relationship for reassurance and rejuvenation. Should his penis perk up from the novelty, he might conclude his marriage to be faulty, dissolve it, and move into a September affair, attempting to begin again. His wife, meanwhile, is coming to grips with her menopause, a seldom celebrated event, with whatever symbolic significance it has for her. In a situation which cries out for a renewal of contact, each partner may be too preoccupied with his own problems to be of much help to the other. The tendency to look outside, to those ever-greener pastures, is often more tempting than a constructive gazing together at a mutual life to be lived and shared. The marked upsurgence in the divorce rate at this hurdle testifies to a series of failures and disillusionments, many of which were misunderstood.

While marriage has its singular joys and ecstatic moments, it should not be forgotten that strains, stresses, and problems are a normal and integral part of this ongoing process. There are times when a man must "ride it out" rather than ride away, and focus on the totality rather than the detail. When normal stress is reacted to as a pathological plague, when outside or professional assistance is eschewed by a do-it-yourself mentality, unnecessary divorces take place, with their quota of misery, impoverishment, and heartbreak for the man, his wife, and his children.

Before the rash divorce, before opting for the heaviest game of Hot Cockles, a man or his spouse should attempt a rational assessment of the marriage. If there is a commonality of aims and objectives; a commitment to "making it work"; an element of enjoyment; a reasonable degree of sexual satisfaction; compatible value systems; and a relative absence of reality stresses, the marriage is a fundamentally sound one. If a man has this type of marriage and is still contemplating a divorce, he should consider seeking professional help first. If, on the other hand, the balance sheet shows a severe deficit, a speedy disengagement might be called for, since many neuroses are kept hot and alive via neurotic marriages. Getting out while the getting's good has preserved the sanity of many a cockled gamesman.

### Instant Replay

Marriage is not Shangri-La. Its capacity to serve as an oasis of affection, consideration, and security is limited in a climate of tumultuous expectations. Rather than an insulated paradise, matrimony emerges as a complex processional, involving a host of unconscious interactions and, not uncommonly, the conflicting needs of the participants.

Disappointed by the absence of angels, some critics now trumpet visions of devils and damnation. While the predators gleefully pontificate on the imminent demise of marriage and family, it might be appropriate for a few hardy souls to address themselves to the reaffirmation and reinforcement of marital bonding, to heal and construct rather than to destroy and to bury a viable patient.

The problem of strengthening the marital bond merits an enormous amount of energy and attention from enormous numbers of people. A few opening suggestions may help to avert a few unnecessary rounds of Hot Cockles.

Since marriage is one of the most crucial moves and involvements in the lives of most people, it should receive at least as much attention in the schools as does trigonometry, French, or *The Canterbury Tales*. There should be mandatory formal education in the processes involved in mate selection and marital interactions. A student who learns to recite *amo, amas, amat,* should also learn that there is more to marriage than romance. This sequence of courses might be included within the curriculum of the humanities or the social sciences, and be conducted with the utilization of both formal lectures and seminar discussions. Since these are to be more than mere rap sessions, the instructors should have adequate training in dynamic psychology and in human relations, drawing upon psychology, sociology, and anthropology for primary source material. Topics such as the Masculine Mystique, matrimonial fantasies, and the role of one's past in marital reactivity would be included. Here, marriage might be divested of such myths as the "instant panacea" and the "eternal undying love." Students might be advised to cultivate a well-thought-out program of mutual activities and interests with their future spouses to prevent the growing apart which infests too many marriages. Didacticism does not change a man's psyche, but it might create a few mental pigeonholes, enabling some to be more aware of what they are doing and perhaps have some hint as to why they are doing it.

Some modifications in societal attitudes must be effectuated. The concept of marriage as a select and specialized institution, which no one should feel pressured to enter, should be encouraged. The bald fact is that many people are unsuited for even a moderately successful marriage. Let society recognize that no marriage is preferable to a bad marriage, and consequently remove the stigma attached to singlehood, just as the Gay Liberation Movement is attacking the social stigma attached to homosexuality. Those who opt not to marry might choose any alternative life style which harms no one, free of social prejudice and disapprobation.

Premarital living together should be encouraged rather than frowned upon. The adage that "you never know someone until you live with them" is more than folk knowledge, it is unvarnished truth. If marriage is to be strengthened, let's stop the mistakes early in the game, preferably before the nuptials. Since more than 50 percent of engaged couples enjoy premarital sexual relations anyway, the likelihood of this suggestion re-creating Sodom and Gomorrah is rather unlikely. This proposal might also allow postponing marriage until the couple is surer and more mature, help to keep the birth rate in check, and legitimize necessary and healthy sexual experimentation.

A campaign should be waged to resurrect the extended family system as a needed and healthy adjunct to the nuclear family. Greater efforts should be expended to bring grandparents back into the community, to increase their sense of participation, and to enhance their self-respect. With a greater sense of vitality and self-esteem, their contacts with their children and grandchildren might be enlivened, and the latter might be more ready to extract and utilize some of the wisdom accumulated by their elders during the span of a lifetime. Likewise, contacts with siblings, cousins, aunts, and uncles should be encouraged where possible, even by an occasional letter or telephone call where distance obtrudes, to enable the couple and their progeny to feel part of a network.

A man should know as much about the marital institution and the nature of his personal involvement as is humanly possible. Then, it is hoped, he will become a referee rather than a participant in Hot Cockles, and the game might, in fact, be finally terminated as the sixteenth-century anachronism it really is.

# 7
# The Crunch

INEVITABLY, THE PHANTASMA of the Masculine Mystique collides with the actualities of the average man's existence. The irresistible fantasy confronts the immovable reality and, with the collision of the juggernauts, the male finds himself caught in the Crunch, squeezed between the jaws of a cosmic vise.

The Mystique, extolling a heroic independence, a sequence of courageous confrontations met by achievement and exploits, has shown no evidence of relaxing its imperatives. Theodore Roosevelt's "Man in the Arena" thesis might serve as a prototype. Roosevelt exhorted: "The credit belongs to the man who is actually in the arena, whose face is marred with sweat and dust and blood; who strives valiantly; who errs and comes short again and again; who knows the great enthusiasms, the great devotions, and spends himself in a worthy cause; who, if he wins, knows the triumph of high achievement; and who, if he fails, at least fails while daring greatly, so that his place shall never be with those cold and timid souls who know neither victory nor defeat." Following this thesis, man's life is a never-ending gladiatorial contest on the blood-spattered sands of the arena. Lest they be considered a relic of those derring-do days of the early twentieth century, it should be noted that these words have been admiringly invoked by Presidents Kennedy and Nixon, and serve as the dramatic highlight of the Broadway hit, *That Championship Season*.

The opposing jaw of the vise, the prosaic and frequently piddling actualities of man's day-to-day experience, appear pallid by contrast. Most men, after all, can only realistically strive to gain an extra inch or to climb a few more rungs on a seemingly limitless ladder. High achievement is highly uncommon, a statistical fluke which few attain or even have access to. Perhaps heroism consists, in part, of defying the odds. Even in the most honest of race tracks or casinos, few walk away with the winnings, while the multitude eventually acquiesce to the probabilities. In striving to attain the seductive realm of the Mystique, while skidding on the slippery shoals of his own uncertain world, a man's reach may well exceed his grasp. He hazards fall, failure, and an unflattering blow to his ego.

In place of Henley's challenge to the winds, "I am the master of my fate: I am the captain of my soul," a more insightful man might say, "My mastery is limited by my biology; by the circumstances of my birth and my life; and by a lack of awareness about myself, of my limitations and my potentials."

## Limitations and Liabilities

From the actuarial standpoint, maleness itself must be considered somewhat of a handicap, for men comprise the more vulnerable half of the species. If a male fetus was cognizant and capable of contemplating his future, he might develop survival anxiety early in the game.

Since life seems to consist of one series of probabilities after another, he would be bound to be dismayed and appalled by the statistical disadvantages suffered by men, when compared with women.

Even in the quiet sanctuary of the womb, 12 percent more males than females die before birth, and 25 percent more boys are born prematurely and with more congenital defects than girls. The cleft lips and strictures of the esophagus and rectum are more common in male babies.

At the moment of birth, the male neonate's life expectancy is 7.4 years less than that of a girl, who is born with the probability of a seventy-five-year sojourn on earth. He would have to live more than fifty-seven years before the insurance tables grant him the likelihood of a seventy-five-year survival. Up to the 1900s, the death rate of American women was greater than that of men. Yet the current rate is 75 percent higher for the male, and wives are outliving their husbands by an average of five years. As of the early 1970s, men can expect to live as long as women did thirty years ago.

Inequity plagues the newborn male immediately after surviving the discomfitures of birth. During the first week, he runs a 32 percent greater mortality risk than does his female counterpart. He is more prone to die a crib death, and even though male fetuses tend to tarry in the womb a few extra days, a baby girl's respiratory and circulatory systems are likely to be in better shape. During the first year of life, 21.8 white males, but only 16.3 females, per thousand fail to survive. Baby boys cry more, sleep less, and are more active and demanding. Girls smile more, and no wonder, with more to smile about!

In the nursery and through their early school years, boys are more likely to evidence speech and reading disorders and are more apt to exhibit a hyperactivity syndrome than girls. Girls are more proficient in speech and are toilet-trained earlier than boys.

Assuming that the fledgling male survives these early hazards, what might he look forward to? Men have a 300 to 400 percent greater chance of leaving this vale of tears through homicide or suicide than do women, and their cancer rate tops the female's by 40 percent. Men are more prone to leukemia, cancer of the skin, larynx, bladder, kidney, stomach, central nervous system, lymphatic system, and lungs. Of course, a man could always give up smoking and concentrate on booze instead, but even alcohol has its sex-linked hazard. Four times as many men are labeled "heavy drinkers" than women. Perhaps they are also more affected by it. For example, ethyl alcohol is metabolized to acetaldehyde by the body, and the latter is more potent than alcohol itself. Male mice given alcohol throw off several times more acetaldehyde in their breath than female mice. Castrate the male, and his acetaldehyde level equals that of the female. Might this not pertain to humans as well? An exorbitant price one pays for life's little pleasures!

Persistence in living introduces the male in his early twenties to arteriosclerosis or hardening of the arteries. It is virtually absent in women until they have passed forty. Death rates from heart disease are three to four times greater for men in the forty-five- to sixty-four-year age bracket, where the overall mortality rate of white males is double that of white women. To add a few psychiatric fillips, the male is three times more vulnerable to obsessive-compulsive neurosis, and five to ten times more prone to become a psychopathic personality; and, as far as sexual deviations are concerned, I suggest a remembrance of "The Sex Life of a Penis." How many female exhibitionists or voyeurs does the average pedestrian encounter?

The idea that all men are created equal is a fanciful, well-intentioned fairy tale. They are obviously born with different levels of biological potentials, which merit neither shame nor apology. However great these discrepancies may be, they are slim in comparison to the disproportion in survival potential between men and women. Biologically, women emerge with survivorship nestled between their bosoms. Yet the Mystique, having little stomach for statistics, urges the male to flex his biological resources, to strain his not unlimited capacities, to emulate the Neanderthal Ideal, and to finally collapse from the Crunch.

In its obsession with performance and achievement, the Mystique is seemingly oblivious to the circumstances surrounding each individual man's birth and development. In their self-assessments, men rarely take these Mystique-discounted contingencies into account. But, as W. C. Fields snortingly advised: "Let's grab the bull by the tail and face the situation."

The male fetus greets the world as a tiny, helpless, illiterate, and barely formed hunk of protoplasm. His inheritance, his genetic makeup, is already fixed, and at this stage of medical progress he can't do a thing to change it. The family he enters is also an established entity. It will be incumbent upon them to nurture, protect, socialize, and educate him. But who are "they" and what are "they" like? Where do they stand socially and financially? Infant mortality, for example, is 50 to 100 percent higher if one's parents are in the lowest socioeconomic segment. What is their attitude toward the newcomer? Was he wanted; were they selecting girls' names instead of boys', and what is their approach to child rearing? Is the father an adequate male to identify with, or is he one of those passive and distant fellows?

Will the mother be overprotective or domineering? If she is indulgent and lacks discipline, her son may turn out infantile, demanding, and always expecting instant gratification. On the other hand, neurosis, submission, anxiety, and inhibitions may menacingly loom if she is too domineering. Where does one draw the line? How will these situations affect his "valiant striving" or his "great enthusiasms"?

To further complicate matters, like Henry Higgins, the fetus is born with his own spark of the divine fire, a temperament of his own. If his parents are quiet souls, how will they react to a robust and tumultuous son? On the other hand, if the boy happens to enjoy a certain contemplative serenity, will he be a comfort or a disappointment? The possibilities and permutations are staggering enough, but the boy must somehow muddle his way through them, saddled with the Mystique.

While parents exert their appropriate and time-honored influence upon their child, the birth order of the boy has its own influences and inducements to weave into his psychic tapestry. If the newborn happens to be the first child, his chances of achievement and eminence soar. The majority of listings in *Who's Who*, the bulk of American scientists, and most of the Rhodes and National Merit Scholars are first or only children. The top 1 percent of I.Q. scorers are also primarily the first or the only, as are college students on both graduate and undergraduate levels. Apparently the first-born gets an initial boost up the ladder. But most boosts have some backlash. Alfred Adler referred to the first-born as "power-hungry conservatives," and a craving for power thrusts the child directly into the path of the Mystique's Dominance Drive. Since the first child has a stake in maintaining the status quo, he tends to be morally and politically more conservative than his rebellious younger siblings. When Gilbert and Sullivan wrote that every man alive was born a liberal or a conservative, they were not far from the mark. How much choice, or "free will," does the growing male really have? Isn't the freedom of decision and action inherent in the Mystique's Heroic Imperative? The first-born also has a more highly developed conscience, is more curious and cooperative, and is more likely to volunteer for psychological experiments. He is also most likely to enlist in the service of the Mystique.

If the newborn has one or more predecessors, his life style might be significantly different. Youngest children are the family "babies," tend to remain so, and are candidates for more than their fair share of attention. They are more likely to become actors, constantly amassing applause and recognition in their lifelong quest to monopolize the limelight. The youngest achieve greater renown, are more likely to be found in college, and have a greater probability of winding up on top of the I.Q. heap than do the middles.

In the unhappy event that the fetus emerges as a middle child, he might reconsider and remain in the unpressured womb indefinitely. Pushed down by their seniors and constantly challenged by their juniors, the middles feel a sardinelike psychic squash. Special tribute should be paid to successful middle children; they've made it against the odds, and with no discernible positional advantage working for them.

Other preexisting determinants envelop the newborn, waiting to shape his future personality and to influence his attainments. Consider his family's socio-economic status, as an example, going beyond the obvious differences in social and material advantages which define affluence and poverty. A boy born to the upper class, who has therefore a lessened likelihood of homicide, psychosis, or suicide, has a 400 percent greater chance of being referred for psychiatric help by his family physician should psychological problems arise. A boy entering a middle-class milieu is most likely to suffer the Achiever Complex, to be caught in the bind between the surge for upward mobility, skyward to the upper class, and the statistical improbability of making it. "Rags to riches" is a rarity, and relatively few Chevrolet and Plymouth purchasers ultimately become possessors of Continentals or Cadillacs, but many knock themselves out trying. Or dwell upon the psychology of the socio-economically deprived youngster. Facing economic hardship and a much higher probability of a broken home, brittle family relationships, and an absentee father, the mere struggle for existence becomes a major preoccupation, and the niceties of psychological development may become negligible or coarsened in the process. Growing up deprived also often means growing up with little impulse control. Since the capacity to internalize one's impulses is a prerequisite for progress, handicaps mount. Fragmented families frequently germinate rage-filled children; and rage plus poor impulse control equals confrontation with the law. A sorry case, calling for any bright innovations which a boy's nimble brain can devise. But, as Reissman and others have demonstrated, the boy's brain will not be working for his best advantage. Thus, as a member of the impoverished, he is more likely to have a visual rather than an aural orientation, which will cause problems in classroom lectures and in following verbal instructions; to develop an external stance rather than becoming introspective, which will diminish his creativity; to center around content rather than form, allowing him to lose the forest for the trees; to become problem-centered rather than being comfortable with abstract thinking (a way-farer in our complex world is lost without the capacity for abstract thought); to develop a spatial rather than a temporal conceptualization, making time relatively unimportant; and to be more expressive than instrumental, allowing for the perception of misery, but lacking the wherewithal to do much about it. He thus develops with an orientation precisely opposite to that required to improve his inherited lot.

It is difficult not to be impressed with the power and the tenacity of the "givens" with which one is born and the difficulty in modifying them. The male fetus enters the world with genes which have already determined how attractive or unattractive he'll appear, what his intelligence level will approximately be, and hundreds of other entities which the medical profession is only now dimly sensing. His maleness decreases his life span and makes him more vulnerable to one catastrophe after the other. The family constellation into which he has been injected has an immeasurable influence on the world outlook and personality he will develop. Their socio-economic position will help determine not only his health, opportunities in the world, and his entire life style, but will also affect his thinking processes.

Although the doctrine of predestination is lately out of style, it is evident that men are born with more rigidities and limitations than the Mystique would admit to. It is equally evident that some men create greater latitudes and options for themselves than do their peers. The "givens" in a man's life are not absolutes, but rather define the likely scope, framework, and patterns of response which he brings into each unique or challenging experience. Patterns can be modified and obstacles overcome by dint of intelligence, effort, and perseverance, but only a rare soul (if he exists at all) can totally divest himself of his "givens" and conform to that pure masculine essence envisioned by the Mystique.

One could argue that it is perhaps best that men remain unaware of the "givens" in their lives, that the knowledge of them might induce a sense of discouragement, a feeling of "what's the use of trying," and a regression to fate, karma, and other forms of resignation. But modifications can be made, and these can best be effectuated with knowledge. Any gambler should know the odds, even those of making an inside straight. Socrates said that the unexamined life is not worth living. Well, that's putting it a bit strong, but the examined life is probably better lived, and an examination of the "givens" of one's life, contrasted with the absurdities of the Mystique, might soften the Crunch.

## The Symptoms

Having lived with the Mystique all their lives, men barely notice the Crunch. Like primitives chronically infested with parasites, they accept weakness and debilitation as a "natural" part of their lives. "If we knew, all the gods would awake," wrote Guillaume Apollinaire; but few are aware, and the gods continue their sleep. The symptoms of the Crunch are so pandemic, and men have become so habituated to them, that they are rarely recognized until the squeeze begins to pinch and the hurt is registered. The ache may appear in the physical, psychic, or psychosomatic spheres, but since men have been programmed to respond only to the obvious and painful wound ("little boys don't cry," and brave men barely wince), a relatively painless malignancy is allowed to develop and to spread until it is ripe to destroy its host.

Consequential to his service as the family emissary

to the outer world, the male most directly confronts change, economic upheaval, social pressure, and similar stresses. Even in a family with shared responsibilities, it is usually the male who must bear that ultimate and final survival responsibility, the last stop in the passage of the buck. Postponement, relaxation, or extra hours of rest, recreation, or diversion on a weekday afternoon are denied most men for the entirety of their working lives. It is frequently the unremitting pressure, the unending insecurity, or the unrelenting monotony which produces the steady influx of stress that eventually exhausts whatever coping mechanisms a man possesses.

Perhaps it is premature to adequately discuss the physical effects of the Crunch upon men. Medical investigation is still primarily occupied with the collection of data. But a few of the more notorious syndromes might be mentioned as they relate to the Mystique.

There is little doubt that the stress of daily living wreaks its toll of coronaries upon the hearts of men, but knowledge of exactly how this is accomplished, and to what extent stress is culpable, await further investigation. We know that men stand a 500 percent greater risk of a coronary than women, and, in the past two decades, deaths from heart attacks have jumped 14 percent among men aged twenty-five to forty-four, while declining by some 8 percent among women in the same age group. Estrogen protects the woman, but does stress condemn the man? An elevation of the blood level of cholesterol has long been recognized as a major factor in increasing the probability of a coronary. When the cholesterol levels of a group of accountants were monitored during a year, their cholesterol was observed to steeply rise from mid-March through mid-April, corresponding to the stress of the tax season. Corporate accountants, whose deadlines occurred at the year's end, showed no spring elevation. It is rather unlikely that this relationship between work stress and elevated cholesterol levels is confined to the accounting profession. A coronary-prone behavior pattern has been delineated by Rosenman, Friedman, and others. Characterized by intense striving for achievement, competitiveness, aggressivity, impatience, a preemptive speech pattern, and a constant awareness of the pressure of time and responsibility, the candidate for a coronary is a living embodiment of the ideals of the Mystique.

Or consider peptic ulcers, 90 percent of which erode the delicate mucosal linings of men's duodena. The duodenal ulcer is primarily a disease of "civilized" man. Indonesians and Bantus rarely develop one, while the high-income administrator or professional living in an urban area is the major target, almost as if social "success" itself drilled a hole into the upper bowel of the man at the top. The man with the ulcer is often caught between desires for dependency and passivity, and an overcompensatory drive for success. The conflict, if enacted on a gut level, digs the ulcer crater. Although ulcer symptoms are noteworthy for their subsidence during vacations, it is precisely the ulcer personality who refuses to take one. He too exemplifies the model of compliance to the directives of the Mystique. Air traffic controllers add an additional dimension to the man-stress-ulcer syndrome. More than 85 percent of air traffic controllers, under the constant stress of making instantaneous life-and-death decisions, show clinical symptoms of peptic ulcers, while 32.5 percent have visible evidence of that ulcerous niche on barium X-rays. An extreme example? Of course. Does it have applicability to other men? Probably.

The riddle of hypertension (high blood pressure) has not been solved. Its causation, probably multifaceted,

likely includes the stress factor. Hokanson's experiments
have demonstrated a relationship between hostility and
hypertension. Pairs of college students had their fingers
attached to electric shocking devices, which allowed one
to give a shock to the other. The subjects who received
a series of shocks evidenced a rise in their blood pressures. If the shockee could then shock his shocker in
return, his blood pressure fell. If this retaliation was pre-
vented, his blood pressure remained elevated for a longer
period of time. How many men, with their livelihoods,
families, or careers at stake, have had to sit by and "take
it," without having the means or the capacity to exact
revenge or to rectify a grievance? What effect has it had
upon their arteries?

Moving from the psychosomatic to the psychic, suicide, the tenth major cause of death in the United States,
emerges as an additional male prerogative. Men commit
suicide three times more frequently than women,
although the latter make more attempts. Either men are
more skilled in killing themselves, or they have more to
kill themselves about. The suicide rate in California,
however, 80 percent higher than the national average of
10.6 to 11.1 suicides per 100,000 population, is recently
showing its greatest increase among women and the
young. In a report prepared by that state's Department of
Public Health, the rise in female suicide is partly attrib-
uted to the gains of the Feminist Movement, and it quotes
Walter Gove in *Sex, Marital Status, and Suicide* on the
price women are paying for entering man's wonderful
workaday world: "Their drive for success and recognition
has increased pressures and opened more possibilities for
failure. In precisely those areas where liberated women
are making the most progress, the male-female suicide
ratio moves toward 'equality.'" The implication is that if

women lived as men do, they too would be more prone to take their own lives. A rather sobering and somewhat distressing postulate for men to ponder while they placate the Mystique! In my professional experience with men who have attempted suicide, I have been impressed by those who had simply been overwhelmed by the Crunch, who saw themselves as "failures," as significantly less than their ideal selves, the never-to-be heroes or Supermen. Their achievement had fallen far short of their needlessly extreme levels of aspiration. After flagellating themselves for their presumptive inadequacies, and depressed by the evaporation of any semblance of self-esteem when the unfortuitous circumstance arose (loss of job, fall in stock market, etc.), suicide became their ultimate sacrifice upon the altar of the Mystique. The fact that survival might be of greater moment than the Mystique's imperatives had somehow gotten lost within the jaws of the Crunch.

These are but some of the more egregious expressions of the Crunch. The drive for achievement found among sufferers from gout, or the diminution of testosterone production in men under stress, might also be mentioned, along with the dozens of illustrations embedded in the preceding chapters on work, sex, and marriage. Each man, upon reflection, can add his own syndromes to what appears to be an interminable list.

The Crunch is the consequence of the Mystique's misperception of the male as a creature of infinite potentials and inexhaustible capacities. Since men, as a group, have not yet attained these deific characteristics, and the individual man is blessed with his own individuality, a unique blend of the superb and the limited, a sense of rational perspective is required for a semblance of satisfactory survival.

During the past decade, women have become aware of some of the incongruities of their life situation and have embarked on a movement to rectify them. Before confronting the issue of male survival, it might be helpful to examine the feminist experience as a possibly helpful prototype for the liberation of the male.

# 8

# From Adam's Rib to Women's Lib

*Cleopatra's Complaint*
*(with an eye toward Shakespeare)*

"LIFE WITH CAESAR grates me. I seem the fool when I am not, while Caesar will be himself. Ten thousand harms, more than the ills I know, my idleness doth hatch. I'm too indulgent. When I was green in judgment, I made great Caesar lay his sword to bed. He plough'd me and I cropp'd, and now I have Caesarion. I have a man's mind, but a woman's might, and this might is expended on the care of his child. While he doth bestride the narrow world like a Colossus, I take Caesarion to play by the Nile. Why should Caesar's name be sounded more than mine? He loves no plays, he hears no music, and he seldom smiles. Is it accepted that I should know no secrets that appertain to him? Am I myself, but, as it were, in sort of limitation, to keep him at meals, comfort his bed, and talk to him sometimes? Dwell I but in the suburbs? I was born free as Caesar. We both fed as well. And now this man has become a god, and Cleopatra is a wretched creature, and must bend her body if Caesar but carelessly nod at her.

"He's a strumpet's fool, while I ofttimes am cunning past man's thought. What conquests brings he home?

When the fit was on him, I did mark how he did shake—
'tis true this god did shake. Ye gods, it doth amaze me a
man of such feeble temper should so get the start of the
majestic world! It is the part of men to fear and tremble.
Whose fortunes rise higher, Caesar's or mine? The fault
lies not in our stars, but in ourselves, that we women are
underlings. Every woman has in her own hands the power
to cancel her captivity. I have immortal longings in me."

Two thousand years have passed, and the complaint
remains unchanged. In the last decade, it has become
more strident and insistent. Rather than the plaintive cry
of an isolated woman, it has now become the liturgy of
the Women's Liberation Movement (WLM). No longer
content to play second fiddle in the masculine symphony,
WLM is demanding at least equal time on the podium.
Marriage, motherhood, and family will no longer suffice.
The human potential is too vast, while the feminine possibilities are too narrow. If man and woman are born free
and equal, why should it be the female who is fettered!

Blessed with the benevolence of the media, which
recognizes a provocative and marketable theme when it
appears, and riding on the inherent righteousness of its
cause, WLM has captured the attention of a nation and
has most certainly aroused its conscience and awareness.
Newspapers, magazines, and television and radio programs besiege the frequently embattled woman with
blandishments that she is no longer simply a woman. She
should now consider herself a socio-political entity in an
army of her sisters, and that army is now on the march.
Archaic institutions are to be toppled, new horizons are
at one's fingertips!

But, as Machiavelli advised his Prince: "There is
nothing more difficult to take in hand, more perilous to

conduct, or more uncertain in its success, than to take the lead in the introduction of a new order of things." Any movement, to be effective, requires a historical perspective, a set of basic assumptions, a coherent philosophy, and a fundamental agreement on methods and goals. The lack of agreement on these issues within the movement is responsible for much of the confusion and misunderstanding in the minds of both men and women when they attempt to seriously address themselves to what the movement is trying to say. WLM is still amorphous in form, wrapped in rhetoric, and in need of a cohesive consensus. There are a multitude of organizations and personalities with ofttimes wide divergencies of assumptions, purposes, and philosophies, despite the very broad areas of commonality. In attempting to discuss WLM, one is certain to alienate various groups within the movement on particular issues. Group A will demur: "But that's *not* what *we're* about." True, but then Group B will counter: "That's *precisely* what we're talking about." And so it goes on issue after issue. With this as prelude, a survey of the WLM spectrum might be assayed, acknowledging that it is descriptive of no one particular organization within WLM, but rather a prospectus of the wide range of the movement and its broad configuration.

## The Genesis

We appear to be in the second upsurgence of the feminist groundswell which began in the middle of the nineteenth century, in the United States. Hobbled by their legal status as chattel, women began to take an active role in the Abolition Movement in the 1830s, much like our current female generation became activists in the Civil Rights Movement in the late 1950s and 1960s. Susan

B. Anthony, Lucretia Mott, Elizabeth Stanton, and Lucy Stone, all heroines of WLM, were actively involved in the abolition of slavery. Here they acquired experience in organization, in philosophizing on a practical level, in holding public meetings, and in dealing with the slings and arrows which inevitably came their way. Their accumulated experiences naturally gave the needed impetus for demanding rights for women, just as they were demanding humanity for slaves.

A meeting of 250 women in Seneca Falls, New York, in 1848 marked the official beginning of political organization for women. The legal position of these women was both pitiable and atrocious. In the 1840s, women became "civilly dead" when they married. They had no control over the use their wages or their estates were put to, since they were legally chattel to their husbands, and were treated as little more than minors by the law. The "Statement of Sentiments," drafted by the Seneca Falls meeting was the feminist parallel to the Declaration of Independence, written only seventy-two years previously. Among its resolutions was the demand for women's suffrage. While seemingly innocuous today, this petition for women's right to vote was a bold move, made by what seems to have been a remarkable group of women with determined leadership qualities. The fight for women's suffrage dominated the Feminist Movement from 1848 through 1920, when the Nineteenth Amendment was at long last passed by the Congress.

Their goals achieved, the Feminist Movement waned. Those women still active within the movement were instrumental in the passage of child labor legislation, a fight for better conditions for working women, and similar social legislation. In the meantime, the growth of women's colleges such as Wellesley, Vassar, Bryn Mawr, and Smith in the generation following Seneca Falls was producing educational opportunities for an elite group of women.

The post–World War I period, an era of relaxed sexual restraints, gave way to the Depression and World War II. Society, shifting gears, became more interested in basic survival than in sexual reform. But the Second World War brought more women out of their homes and into the labor force; and a trend, like a tax, once established, seldom simply fades into oblivion. While the 1950s seemed rather quiescent, the 1960s saw women again drawn into political activism, this time in the Civil Rights Movement. The time for the second upsurgence of the Feminist Movement, the Women's Liberation Movement, had come and was officially proclaimed by the publication of Betty Friedan's *The Feminine Mystique* in 1963.

It is always tempting to play the "Why now?" game, especially when sex is involved. Why should the Feminist Movement have so suddenly been resurrected, sparkling and flaming like an everlasting Roman candle, in a period in which women have made more advances in a generation than they had since the rape of the Sabine women? A congruence of felicitous factors seems to have occurred in the early 1960s which made it all but inevitable.

Involvement in the Civil Rights Movement replicated the experiences of the early feminists in the Abolition Movement. The moral impetus of civil rights for Negroes was easily enlarged to include the "liberation" of women. Note the use of the word "liberation," with its slavery antecedent. "Instability" was becoming increasingly more descriptive of our society, and "polarization" (racial, ethnic, labor-management, etc.) was in the air. Why not add male-female to the polemics of polarization? Furthermore, women were granted the gift of time. With increased mechanization of household chores, more time became available for considerations, interests, and activities outside the home. Consequently, women who previously had never been compelled to work for economic reasons were to be found within the labor force, increasingly experiencing themselves as competent professionals. With the sense of immediacy underscored by a "see it now" media, "activism" or action became more natural, more reflexive. The "affluent generation," the better-educated and better-cared for children of the World War II generation, were less concerned with a reasonably assured survival and more concerned with the quality of their increased life span. Finally, reform tends to increase the pressures for further reform. If women had achieved so many rights and advances, why stop now? Press on to "complete equality"! An "idea whose time had come" had arrived. Now, what is to be done with it?

## The Assumptions

Any movement, be it a revolution, a crusade, a sales campaign, or a political party preparing its platform, must be based on a set of assumptions, implicitly or explicitly stated. For example, the perennial political cry, "Throw the rascals out!" assumes: 1) The party in power is comprised of a bunch of crooked rascals. 2) The country, state, or city would benefit by the removal of these rascals from office. Of course this need not be the case. It might be better governed by intelligent rascals than by honest fools, but the assumption of the beneficent result of the removal of rascality still remains. 3) The party struggling to obtain power is devoid of rascality and will provide honesty, integrity, and political genius for the foreseeable future, if the electorate would only cooperate.

The Women's Liberation Movement has its constellation of assumptions as well. Their data and documentation, have already been the subjects of a tidal wave of books. A simple review of some major assumptions that reappear with notable frequency and/or intensity might suffice.

Boys and girls, maintain the feminologists, are born with little or no sexually differentiating features other than their reproductive apparatus. The differences one discerns in the temperament, personality, and social roles between men and women are the result of "socialization" or "brainwashing" perpetrated by a society which imprints its distorted concepts of masculinity and femininity on impressionable and previously unstructured minds. This "brainwashing" is accomplished via our current child-rearing practices, our educational methods, and by the very structure of society itself. This thesis has a philosophical kinship with John Locke, the philosophical apostle of the Revolution of 1688. In his famed exposition of the *tabula rasa*, Locke says: "Let us then suppose the mind to be, as we say, white paper, void of all characters, without any ideas; how comes it to be furnished?" WLM has its rather definitive answer, at least in the male-female categories.

Women as a class are discriminated against by society in the vocational and educational spheres. In the vocational area, positions of status, responsibility, and power are all but exclusively male preserves. Adding insult to injury, women receive less pay for doing the same work that a man does, despite equality of performance and aptitude.

Educationally, the "prestige" subjects, the natural sciences, medicine, law, and engineering, are traditionally "masculine subjects," while women seem consigned to the humanities, which provide minimal opportunities for social advancement. The men take Business Administration, while the women piddle with Home Economics. Furthermore, as one climbs the educational ladder, the number of women in responsible faculty positions magically declines, diminishing the number of successful female-role models for girls to identify with.

The roles which our society delegates to woman dehumanize and stultify her personality. Her potentials as a human being, while equal to, or possibly greater than, man's, are throttled, since she is only allowed the status of a sex object or an economic slave to the man.

The oppressive subjugation of women has not simply occurred by chance, but reflects some Grand Patriarchal Scheme, which allows men to retain their preeminent position. Thus men become the major enemies of women. This hypothesis assumes a tacit conspiracy, consensually agreed upon, not only by the males inhabiting this planet at this particular time, but by all males who have lived through the preceding millennia.

Man-woman relationships are basically power transactions ("Sexual Politics") in which all the trump cards reside with the male. The presupposition is that mutual affection, regard, or love, if they exist at all, are either illusory, delusional, or of minuscule import when viewed against the background of an awesome power struggle. This was affectionately phrased by Ti-Grace Atkinson when she defined "love" as "the victim's response to the rapist."

Our culture incorporates a grossly and hideously distorted image of female sexuality, with its whore-madonna dichotomy, its negative reaction to the female genitalia ("cunt," "gash," "snatch," etc.), and its unrealistic emphasis on passivity as the female's "natural" sexual role.

The institution of marriage is harmful to women, and consequently should be eschewed. It is little more than a devilish device designed to ensure their continued subjugation. It infantilizes the woman, and continues her status as chattel. The image of the "happy homemaker" is mostly myth, concocted by imperious males and fostered by innocent imbeciles.

The family structure, as presently constituted, is passé and dysfunctional. It entraps women in a condition of quasi-servitude, and is an ineffective child-rearing institution which visits the psychopathology of the parents and society upon the offspring and denies fundamental human rights to minors. The present-day family structure may be replaced by numerous alternatives which effectively do away with a pernicious patriarchy which has done a devastating disservice to both women and children.

Along with the liberation of women, men would achieve liberation as well. Their constant need to prove their virility and power, their machismo, would be reduced, with the consequent easing of the pressured existence which is their lot.

Women allow their oppressed condition to continue because: 1) they are insufficiently aware of its existence, and are therefore in need of "consciousness raising"; and 2) they fear the freedom that would follow their liberation, in much the same manner as long-term prison inmates fear the "outside" and opt for a return to the penitentiary.

The Women's Liberation Movement is beset by enemies, who are defined by Germaine Greer as "the doctors, psychiatrists, health visitors, priests, marriage counselors, policemen, magistrates and genteel reformers."

The lesbian alternative is a volitional choice made by women revolting against their passive role in a patriarchal society.

The world would be better off without men. All-female communes or the "ultimate solution" of Miss Solanas, previously discussed, are certainly worthy of consideration.

The time has arrived for the women in our society to throw off the yoke of oppression and transform our society. This is to be accomplished *now*, in a revolutionary rather than an evolutionary fashion. The patriarchal power structure will surrender none of its prerogatives voluntarily. It must be actively challenged and shaken. Evolution is a notoriously slow and chancy process. Ergo, a more radical revolutionary tactic is called for. If the deed be done, do it now!

While the above hypotheses do not completely cover the entire WLM spectrum, they do represent many of the preeminent sentiments voiced by the activists within the movement. Given a set of hypotheses, it is incumbent upon an effective organization to adopt some philosophical stance and develop a coherent system of purposes and aims. If one thinks of a philosophy as a necessary system which a person forms for the conduct of his or her life, the Women's Liberation Movement must have a similar system from which to formulate its goals.

There appear to be three major political philosophies whirling within the WLM orbit, all of which are currently in flux. They vary with the inclination of their prime spokeswomen, and with the evolutionary processes within the various organizations of WLM.

The more conservative position accepts the necessity and, indeed, the desirability of maintaining the societal status quo, but advocates appropriate reforms within the system to bring more justice, status, and opportunity to women. Our social order would thus be maintained, but the role of women would be enhanced, with full equality with men in the social, political, legal, and vocational spheres. NOW, the National Organization for Women, is the best-known representative of this approach, and officially speaks for several thousand women. It has advocated increased involvement of women in the affairs of their community and in the government at large, outright repeal of abortion laws, equality of vocational opportunities, etc.

The more radical elements within WLM find the conservative position too bland in its aims and too placatory in its approach methodology. They aim at either the complete transformation of society or its actual overthrow to actuate more extreme feminist goals. Their political positions run the gamut from apolitical, to various forms of socialism, through Maoism, and finally to a leaderless anarchy. Accepting the aims of the conservative group as less than a bare minimum, they are more concerned with the complete dissolution of all sex roles, the abolition of marriage, and alternatives to the family unit. Men are seen as "the enemy," and either lesbianism or masturbation are viewed as preferable alternatives to any form of intercourse with men. Ti-Grace Atkinson and her group of Radical Feminists exemplify this position. A headline in the *New York Post* on September 3, 1971, announced: "Ti-Grace Finds the Mafia 'Morally Refreshing,'" and went on to quote her as extolling the Mafia as "the oldest resistance movement in the world—seven centuries of resistance. The value system of the Italian-American community is Mafiosi, and we have a lot to learn from it. It's a revolutionary underground value system that requires a commitment to the death. The government is the enemy, and no one betrays another, no matter what the cost." While this may appear rather extreme, the article notes: "As ever, a familiar refrain is heard again along some frontiers of Women's Liberation: 'Maybe she's right. The thing about Ti-Grace, she's always two years ahead of everybody else.'"

The activities of the radical element are dramatic and media-catching. WITCH, the Women's International Conspiracy from Hell, cast a spell upon the Chase Manhattan Bank; other groups have disrupted the activities of the American Stock Exchange with cries of "Women Power" or "Desexagrate Wall Street." The conservative group, on the other hand, directs most of its energies toward exerting pressures on legislative bodies, business and educational institutions to promote reform.

Obviously, these two positions are not simply separate entities. Their aims and activities commingle at times, and there are numerous feminist groups which occupy intermediate positions. But their common goal is centered on the advancement of the Feminist Movement, unlike the third group.

The third faction consists of those individuals and organizations whose primary interests and concerns focus on issues other than feminism, but have a common concern with WLM and therefore join and utilize it in the pursuit of their own goals. Political groups such as the Socialist Workers Party and S.D.S. would fall into this category, as would the Gay Activists Alliance and the Radicalesbians, to the extent to which the acceptance and promulgation of homosexuality supersedes their concern for the Feminist Movement itself.

## The Goals

The major goals of WLM, from the reasonable to the rampantly radical, might be summarized as follows:

Women's suffrage must be made more meaningful by increased organizational activities directed to producing a larger turnout of voting women who are better informed about the issues that pertain to them.

The formation of powerful political alliances with women of poverty or minority groups, who are seen as doubly victimized by a sexist system.

An end to all war, which is viewed as an expression of the Masculine Mystique that historically uses violence to solve its problems.

The correction of existing inequities in law, education, employment, and our social order that discriminate against women. Thus, "equal pay for equal work" and equal access to job and educational opportunities would become mandatory. Textbooks would be revised to eliminate any vestiges of sexism.

A boycott against institutions or businesses that discriminate against women in employment, advertising, etc., ensuring constant watchfulness against sexist exploitation.

The active encouragement of women to expand their roles beyond the home and the family.

Full economic independence for women. This might involve payment for work done in the home, and would dictate the establishment of government-sponsored day care centers for children.

Full equality with men in the social, vocational, and family spheres. This might require an equal division of all labor between husband and wife.

The abolition of the institution of marriage.

The abolition of the family structure as it exists today.

The radical transformation of society along a variety of lines including: a socialist, Maoist, or anarchist configuration; or the abolition of all sex roles, with the removal of the guarantee of paternity to a particular man; or a complete segregation of women from men; and the establishment of communal structures which would effectuate the preceding items.

The right of women to choose from a variety of life

styles, including lesbianism, promiscuity, and singlehood, without encountering social prejudice.

The total abolition of the male sex, Miss Solanas's ultimate solution, or, at the very least, a total dissolution of all role differences between men and women.

## A Modest Critique

· The Women's Liberation Movement is most certainly more than just a group of dissatisfied women with unconscious penis envy or a sense of biologic inferiority. The old saw that "Anatomy is destiny" is not true. If anything is "destiny," it is character and luck. Many aims and activities of WLM reflect the legitimate protests of an intelligent, determined, articulate, and balanced group of women. The Feminist Movement gives voice to authentic problems women encounter, not only within the American culture, but worldwide. Women, comprising somewhat more than half the human race, are certainly entitled to equal pay for the same work as performed by men, the same right to an unbiased education that men enjoy, and an end to all forms of exploitation predicated on the sexual apparatus which they happened to be born with. The Women's Liberation Movement raises these issues and addresses itself to their rectification. It has pushed for needed reforms, such as the repeal of anti-abortion legislation, that were long overdue. I have no doubt that if men became pregnant instead of women, free abortion would not only have been permitted, but sanctified, centuries ago.

Most people, female and male, suffer an insufficiency of self-respect and self-esteem. The Feminist Movement is actively involved in increasing the quality and quantity of these precious qualities in women. In propagandizing the ideal of a better life, it helps both men and women reach beyond their daily existence. Most particularly, it encourages women to expand their horizons, to see themselves more actively involved in politics, the professions, in higher education, all of which should benefit from their increased participation. In this venture, some women are goaded into abandoning the infantile role bequeathed to them by their families and solidified by their husbands.

WLM has performed important educative functions, providing information on topics as diversified as contraception, the nature and variations of a woman's sexual responses, and the deceptive nature of so much advertising.

In urging the reassessment of the female and male roles in our culture, WLM is a godsend to men if it diminishes their need to maintain artificial images of virility, and might reduce the stress which men live under. The cultural stereotype of women is likewise grossly artificial. It is in dire need of revision.

There are beneficial aspects to the advocacy of increased professionalism in the care of children. Some women simply are miserable mothers, and mother-surrogates would do a much better job with their children. In day care centers, the peer relationships would be a positive influence in a child's life, at least after the age of three, when children actively engage each other. I would question its benefits in this regard prior to the age of two and a half.

Finally, in pointing out alternative life styles, those women who feel themselves ill suited to marriage or motherhood may find the types of existence that best suit their needs. Neither the single life, the lesbian life, nor the woman who elects to have a series of meaningful relationships with men should evoke a raised eyebrow or lowered social esteem. Society should mature beyond that point of pettiness.

However, the Feminist Movement has increased polarization in a society already far too invested in extremes. In a civilization riven by inimical factions, a new discordant note is injected. The "battle of the sexes" is now further intensified by the encouragement of women to view men as their oppressors and their born enemies. How much higher should we raise the temperature of turmoil? Should the female-male relationship be transmuted into an abattoir? Emotional instability is endemic to our culture, ravaging both men and women who barely maintain a sense of intactness. In attacking the fragile identities of many women, by denigrating their roles as wives, mothers, and members of caring family units, WLM may inadvertently increase anxiety and instability in people who require just the opposite.

For many women, quite possibly the majority of women, marriage and family is a truly gratifying and rewarding career. Many elements within WLM negate these satisfactions, as well as others, such as love, romance, and security, with a sneering intolerance. If marriage is nothing but the "oppressive institution" Simone de Beauvoir claims it to be, what viable alternative do we have which will provide the requisite warmth, intimacy, and security so desperately needed in an increasingly dehumanized and alienated society? Why not concentrate on bettering marriage, instead of destroying it? In advocating the dissolution of sex roles in those marriages still extant, WLM is also diminishing the ease and efficiency of function which assigned roles provide in all social organizations. Modification of these roles is meaningful, their dissolution is destructive. Furthermore, in totally negating female-male differences, one ends up with a form of "overkill," encouraging some women to mimic men, and vice versa, in a strained and artificial fashion. Women are more proficient at mothering, and only men can fulfill those paternal functions that are now becoming more clearly defined.

When Germaine Greer blithely advocates the raising of children by paid adults, who never inform the child who its "womb-mother" is, let alone the identity of its father, she betrays a naive and casual disregard of much research in child development undertaken in the past century. An infant has both a psychological and biological need of a warm nutrient relationship with a mother, for at least its first two years. This relationship provides the requisite security and affection to inculcate that sense of safety, adequacy, and positivism which sparks its further development. It provides the infant with the capacities to engage in future peer and societal interactions. Its absence or disruption eventuates in a psychologically crippled human being. I wonder what experience Miss Greer and her disciples have had with war orphans or with adopted children who embark on a lifelong search to discover their "true parents." How many women who propound this solution have children of their own, or if they do, have had anything approaching a positive mothering experience? I seriously question whether an impersonal, even if interested, professional parent-surrogate would provide the affection and information that a healthy natural mother would give to the young child, both qualitatively and quantitatively.

What is to be the fate of the woman who elects to raise her own children? Is she to become a social pariah? We find a higher incidence of antisocial and aggressive behavior in children of disrupted families. Should this disruption be further encouraged, or should we concentrate on increasing family cohesiveness? This irresponsible "shoot from the hip" approach can result in incalculable havoc. The baby is thrown out with the bathwater, and few meaningful targets are hit.

The parent-child relationship has been interpreted by elements of Women's Lib as falling within the dominance-submission pattern of some insidious power structure. Consequently, a concern about the denial of rights to minors has been raised. Let me exclude abnormal circumstances, such as child beating and other forms of obvious brutality visited by disturbed parents upon their children; the social order unequivocally stands opposed to this. Is parenthood, then, only the exercise of dominance? Do love, concern, and tenderness play any role in parental reaction? Why should the child-parent relationship be egalitarian? Does the child need a peer or a parent? "Minors" require a certain structure and discipline to develop as functional human beings in a highly complex society. The overly permissive parent, the parent who is the child's "equal" and "buddy," rears an overly indulged child who cannot adapt to the realities of the world outside the home. Does the minor have the "right" to use heroin, alcohol, or disrupt a classroom? If he doesn't, who is to inform him of that fact? Not his teachers certainly; they get him too late for that, and their job is to teach, not to humanize.

Kate Millett prescribes the end of all sexual inhibitions in adolescent and pre- and extramarital relations. This is more than most young adolescent girls or boys and most marriages can handle. Every society has some set of sexual norms and taboos. Our convoluted culture cannot cavalierly dispense with all of them, at least in the foreseeable future. Most assuredly, many taboos (for example, premarital virginity) should be minimized, mitigated, or totally dispensed with, but not in one sweep of the broom, and not until society has evolved to the point where the change can be effectively incorporated. When the Radicalesbians advocate the lesbian alternative, they propose a life style which more than nine out of ten women would find alien, futile, and unhappy. Antihomosexual legislation, and social and vocational discrimination against the lesbian, are abhorrent from any humane and intelligently informed standpoint, but the propagandizing of homosexuality as the "preferential" life style serves to alienate more women than it attracts.

WLM exaggerates and overestimates the "male role" in our culture, and loses the individual in the process. The individual man simply doesn't have the money, power, or status Women's Lib conjures up as representative of "the male." Everyman is more often a poor soul, desperately trying to hold on, existing marginally economically, powerless in the corporate and political structure, and anxiety-ridden for some semblance of status. Feminist writers frequently present an immature and childlike view of men, akin to a young girl's appraisal of her father. One of the more poignant features of these writings is the infantile depiction of men as free from all difficulties, as inheritors of reward without payment. The leading proponents of WLM are middle-class intellectuals who enjoy established positions in our culture. Miss Greer has a Ph.D. in English, and combines teaching with television and journalism. Miss Millett is a sculptress who has exhibited in New York and Tokyo, has taught literature and philosophy, and is married. Ms. Steinem can always make it as a journalist—pretty legs or no. They might survive the immediate abolition of marriage and family, with its resultant chaos and insecurity. Most women won't. Even Miss Greer admits that what Mrs. Friedan, of NOW, is proposing for women is "free admission to the world of the ulcer and the coronary." Is a woman necessarily happier "out there where the action is," grubbing away like most men? Is it either-or, outside or inside, or can both be satisfactorily combined? "Complete economic freedom" is no more feasible for most women than it is for most men, unless one happens to be extremely well off. All freedoms have their price tags. How much is the average woman willing to pay for what may prove to be only a semantic "freedom"? Ask the man with the coronary before you answer.

While all revolutions must have their devils, WLM has constructed a veritable pantheon of demons—the "Establishment," the capitalist system, men, the police, judges, doctors, psychiatrists, etc. Apparently according to some feminist writers a woman's lot would somehow be improved by the removal of policemen and judges. I suspect that this suggestion would meet with a rather cool reception among women in urban areas, who are rightly clamoring for more police protection and a more efficient court system. The thesis is advanced that women should only accept medical treatment from female family physicians, gynecologists, and psychiatrists, since only female practitioners can adequately empathize with and understand their women patients. Since only 7 percent of physicians in the United States are women, there may be some problem in the distribution of medical care, even assuming a vast increase in the numbers of female physicians in the near future. Using a similar logical framework, the same thesis can be extended to mandate the treatment of children by other children, that only women who have borne children be obstetricians, that the sightless should be treated by the blind, and that only a physician who has himself experienced a coronary occlusion should minister to a man with a heart attack. This is a reductio ad absurdum. One might equally argue that an ardent feminist may be handicapped in realistically handling the problems of a female patient. A physician who treats members of his or her own family may utilize poor judgment. Were one to require surgery, the scalpel might best be wielded by an objective surgeon rather than by an overly involved friend. A patient requires an intelligent, knowledgeable, and interested physician, be that physician male or female.

Many solutions proposed by WLM writers are presently impractical. Many social changes envisioned by the Feminist Movement were tried in Russia after the 1917 Revolution, only to be revoked as unworkable in the 1930s and the 1940s. Even in Communist China, after more than two decades of sexual egalitarian reform, men still do the heavier work and are paid more "work points" and "women's work" still prevails. As of the summer of 1971, of the 170 members of the Chinese Communist Party's Central Committee, only 15 were women. Apparently any society needs time to effectively incorporate major changes into its structures.

Given the multitude of extreme positions and proposals within the Women's Liberation Movement, one should not lose sight of many reasonable and realistic expectations. Those positions most likely to succeed will be balanced responses to complex demands. This evolutionary process will be accelerated and expedited by the more pragmatic members of the Feminist Movement, despite the passionate polemics of its more radical elements. I would recommend Plutarch's suggestion that "perseverance is more prevailing than violence; and many things which cannot be overcome when they are together, yield themselves up when taken little by little."

# 9

# That Matter of Survival

A ZEN PARABLE has a man hanging halfway down the side of a steep escarpment, desperately clinging to a thin vine. On the ground below, a tigress and her hungry cubs await his arrival, salivating with anticipation. Above, two mice, one brown and the other white, gnaw away at the root stalk of his lifeline. An awkward situation. He spies a black orchid blossoming from the cliff wall, a hypnotic palette of iridescent pastels. "How beautiful," he murmurs.

So this cursory sketch of the average male's existential absurdities and trepidations inevitably ends with a portrait of an embattled and endangered species deserving of strenuous efforts at study and conservation. Manipulated by the Mystique, squeezed in the Crunch, the male requires more than token assistance to maintain even a modicum of human function. A civilized survival, in the physical, psychological, and social senses of that primordial term, demands individual and collective ingenuity to devise, learn, and adapt to changed ground rules.

Perhaps we require the concentrated efforts of task forces, academic armadas, and architects of social change for more complete exploration and analysis of the dilemma. But this is obviously dealing in decades. Today's male has but one lone lifetime at his disposal. We must help the poor fellow get off that vine as soon as possible; the blandishments of the orchid will no longer suffice. What can be done in the interim?

Begin with generalizations, attitudes and assumptions, philosophies and psychological sets. We live in a world of particulars and precise directions, but it is premature to be overly involved with the particulars of male survival. The absorption in the particular, the precise placement of the exclamation point and the italic, has plagued the Women's Liberation Movement, for example, fragmenting rather than focusing, producing obfuscation and confusing goals. No, in this embryonic stage, think in terms of themes: of madness and mystique, of males and masculinity, of feminology and female chauvinism, of essence and existence. Leave the exegesis and the implementation of the items to future students and the technicians.

College campuses throughout the United States have overnight become sprinkled with courses in women's studies, a surface dive into the springs of the female experience, with some universities offering it as a major area of study. Wittingly or not, they are creating Feminology as a new field within the Social Sciences. And this is good, personally and educationally, as is anything that broadens the depths of one's self-awareness and perception. Considering the unfortunate and tenuous state of the oppressed male, equal academic treatment is called for. The science of Hominology or Masculinology (or any other suitable Latin- or Greek-derived term) ought to be created and explored. New ideas ought to be injected into the varicosed veins of a static society that often opts for the status quo. "A Survey of Hominology" in academic clothes has its uses: it would attract bright young brains to fertilize the field, and it would produce federal grants, subsidies, and foundation backing, allowing more accurate information to be gathered in a shorter period of time, thereby hastening the moment of salvation. Pecuniary power has been known to influence modifications of the public mind and mores.

The successful survivor, like Sabatini's Scaramouche, should be born with the gift of laughter and the sense that the world is mad. Since most men are not blessed with so beneficent a patrimony, it is incumbent upon them to develop it as rapidly as possible. The term "the sick society" has become an overpopularized cliché. But if some one-third to one-half of the particular individuals in this society are actually psychiatrically sick, it is another matter. Perspective changes when the individual rather than the group is focused upon. This horrendous fact is neither trite, well known, nor sufficiently appreciated, despite a number of epidemiological studies published to substantiate it. One such classic investigation was the Midtown Study, reported in 1962. Under the direction of the late Dr. Thomas Rennie, a sample of 1,660 adults, in the twenty to fifty-nine age range, and living in a heterogeneous area in Manhattan, were surveyed by a multidisciplinary group of social scientists and psychiatrists for evidence of symptomatology, disability, and interference with function due to psychological factors. Only 19 percent were found to be "well." Thirty-six percent showed mild symptom formation, 22 percent evidenced moderate symptom formation, while 23 percent were functionally impaired from a "marked" to a "totally incapacitated" degree. And this from data derived primarily in the 1950s! Considering the multitude of cracks rending the cement of our culture and institutions in subsequent years, one can only shudder at the extensive pathology more current surveys would reveal. Other studies in other areas reveal reasonably similar statistics. Add to this the fact that many family physicians, specialists in internal medicine, and medical and diagnostic clinics maintain that more than 50 percent of patients seen, examined, and diagnosed are found to be suffering primarily from psychiatric disorders. With the $4 billion per year spent on the treatment and the prevention of mental illness, plus the $17 billion lost in the lessened productivity of the mentally ill, the minimal tab of $21 billion per year in the United States provides the financial concommitant to parallel the preceding statistics.

The perception of this social madness can be of primary survival significance. Its recognition better orients a man to the actualities of his environment, diminishing confusion and misunderstanding. It provides a priceless sense of perspective which takes a psychic load off his back. Why remain in a relationship or a marriage that has nothing better than neurotic carping to recommend it, when the fault does not reside within both partners? Why dignify with serious regard the ludicrous challenge, the undeserved insult, or the jealous gibe once they are recognized as the products of someone else's skewed psyche? Best to detach and leave them to Heaven, or to their next victim, or both. The capacity to draw the line between someone else's inanity or insanity and one's own neurosis and culpability is a grace which preserves life, limb, friendship, and humor.

Talent for tolerance correspondingly reduces the obsession with "justice," "fairness," etc., in a culture in which these qualities are more often ideals than realities. Who ever said that life is fair?

The appreciation of the irrational results in a lessening of excessive expectation from others, as well as from oneself, avoiding needless expenditures of energy, anger, self-recrimination, and intestinal turmoil. When defensiveness and hurt are replaced by a modicum of toleration and humor for the irrationality of others, tautness gives way to relaxation. George Bernard Shaw observed that "Life is too short for men to take it seriously."

A man can react to life's irrationalities, conflicts, and contradictions with anger, anxiety, and depression. Or he can develop a sense of humor, an ability to laugh at absurdities within himself and his world, many of which he is powerless to alter. As George Santayana noted: "There is no cure for birth and death save to enjoy the interval." Humor increases the quality of one's survival and lengthens its duration.

The Masculine Mystique may be viewed as one of the major symptoms of social madness, an intrinsic component of warfare, Inquisitions, and other fanciful versions of fanaticism. The male will continue his abysmal suspension so long as the Mystique maintains its grip on him. Most neurotic symptoms once served an adaptational function, the precise nature of which lies buried in the recesses of the afflicted past. With distortion, the passage of time, and the maturation of the individual, these earlier and more primitive adaptive devices become dysfunctional and disabling. In short, what once was useful has now become a sickness.

The Mystique should be regarded as a dysfunctional and distorted vestige, a collective remnant of social exigencies which have outlived their utility, but have acquired an independent existence of their own. For example, in the delicate balance of our social structure today, the Neanderthal Ideal becomes an absolute menace, for if humanity is to survive, it will depend on the development of the cerebral and the containment of brute force.

In prerevolutionary China, the Emperor ruled by virtue of the "Mandate of Heaven," a decree by the Divinities that allowed the ruler to reign as long as he governed wisely and well. If he proved to be a bounder or an incompetent ignoramus and was overthrown, the presumption was that a displeased Heaven had withdrawn its Mandate to reign. Similarly, the Mystique has had its term of potential and power. It is presently fumbling, and should be deposed as expeditiously as possible. As a civilization, we may have sufficiently advanced to proceed with the dissection and the dismemberment of the Mystique, and arrange for the male's reabsorption into the human race.

This may prove to be somewhat of a herculean task for even the best-intentioned. A Mystique which has evolved over many centuries, which has become so integrated in the trivia of everyday existence, will not be cavalierly dispensed with by divine fiat or the wave of some judicial or legislative wand. Nevertheless, the moment of mobilization for its overthrow appears to have arrived. Rather than being heralded by the blare of trumpets, it may well begin with one man whispering: "Why?"

An approach must be formulated, and a methodology devised, to launch the campaign. The single brilliant stratagem or the incisive stroke is probably nonexistent. The Feminist Movement has sought this approach, but to no avail. I doubt that the male will fare any better in this regard, although he can profit from the feminist trials and errors.

The approach of the psychiatrist might be of some value at this juncture. In the treatment of a mental or emotional disorder, it is axiomatic that a disabling symptom routinely accepted by a patient as a normal part of himself, however abnormal it may be, must first be converted into an alien "thing" infesting his psyche. Thus, if a man has been blithely assuming and behaving with the surety that he is Napoleon Bonaparte, the first stage of his treatment would aim at loosening his conviction. The goal of the second stage would be to have him regard his Napoleonic complex as an alien "something" which, for a multitude of reasons, has intruded into his ego. In the third stage, it is incumbent upon the psychiatrist to aid the patient in finding adequate satisfaction in the real world to compensate for whatever needs and lacks his Napoleonic delusion satisfied. Similarly, the Mystique, accepted by men as a perfectly natural part of their lives, must eventually be labeled and treated as an alien and extraneous aberration.

Our campaign of therapeutic reeducation must first delineate the Mystique as a concrete entity within the public mind, define its components, plumb the protean depths of its dimensions, and proceed to describe the insidious and dehumanizing effects of its modus operandi, not only on men, but upon women and the totality of society as well.

At the outset, expect no bursts of impassioned applause, no hurrahs, bravos, or *olés*. Anticipate instead the grudging resistance, the silent avoidance, and the hostile gibe. Men, women, and their society have vast unconscious investments in the Mystique, and might understandably be expected to stoutly defend their perceived interests. It will take patience, perspiration, and perseverance to convince them that their investment is a misplaced and losing proposition.

Society, after all, thrives upon the Achiever Complex as the Hotspur of progress. It looks to the Dominance Drive for a steady supply of politicians, and to serve as a springboard for those with inclinations toward the accretion of power. It relies on the devotion and overexertion of the Provider to produce, to earn, and to borrow the wherewithal to keep the economy overheatedly rolling along with geometric progression. It requires the supermaniacal and heroic masculine ideal to provide the soldiery ready to risk life and limb in warfare, and to produce the spectacle of the male automaton for its panoply, parades, and panache. Indeed, so much of the socially extraneous is ordered around the Mystique that its too sudden demise might be a shock, akin to a momentary transport to the land of Oz. Anticipate social antipathy.

The resistive male will hotly hold to his imagined prerogatives, to the myth of male superiority with its spectre of power and glory. His fantasy of sexual athleticism, of playboy potentials, of the hero who is yet to be, will not readily surrender to such prosaic matters as mere survival. Expect no paeans from many penile possessors.

The female may bemoan the ensuing lack of enthusiasm on the part of the Provider, mourn the loss of the Superman, and nostalgically yearn for those extra efforts of the Sexual Athlete. Those who bask in the reflected sun of the Achiever may lose a bit of their tan. Among women who relish an infantile role, the maturity and responsibility forced upon them by the dissolution of the Mystique will come as bitter medicine.

The most vocal opposition to the ousting of the Mystique will come from both male and female chauvinists. The male chauvinist has been sufficiently caricatured, blasphemed, and vilified, negating any undue influence that he may have possessed. His blatancy has made him a laughable character, and perhaps deservedly so.

The female chauvinist is a different genus, however, and comes in two seemingly opposing species. The militant female chauvinist simply believes that she belongs to the superior sex, and loudly proclaims her conviction. The plight of the male is relatively inconsequential to her. She cares little about the Masculine Mystique, since she doesn't believe in it in the first place.

The other species of female chauvinist, the covert chauvinist, will be a far more subtle and serious antagonist. This species extols the difference between the sexes and demands that cultural male and female stereotypes be maintained. Having thus become the philosophical bed companion to the male chauvinist, she becomes the bosomed and vaginated instrument of the Masculine Mystique. Insisting on the validity of male superiority and supremacy, she correspondingly demands the entire spectrum of female prerogatives predicated on the caricatured weakness, passivity, and helplessness of the female. In her exaltation of the Mystique, she impales the male, not only as her everlasting Provider, Hero, and Achiever, but also as her eternal servitor and supplicant. She can be recognized by her posturing as the consummate female, by her evaluation of men solely in terms of their power and achievement, and by her obscene use of passivity. She demands protection and genteel niceties, and rather than being sincerely flattered by them, expects the male sacrifice as her due, being "only a hapless female." Most psychiatrists have seen her husband, desperate for a divorce, but guilt-ridden beyond reason lest his fragile flower wilt and die should they separate. Yet, after the divorce, she is amazingly adept at quickly fastening on to another victim.

The covert female chauvinist emerges as a formidable antagonist to the liberation and the survival of the male, since the entirety of her life style is predicated on the maintenance of the Masculine Mystique.

Apparently, the Mystique has its awesome array of defenders, numerous and diverse, highly invested and strongly motivated. From the overall strategic standpoint, the defenders must be made aware of the exorbitant price the Mystique exacts from its devotees, a bizarre cost-benefit ratio in which the price paid is far in excess of any benefits conceivably derived.

Society as a whole pays the scathing price of a creaking and crumbling social order. The Mystique can be directly implicated as the prime or the accessory agent behind warfare, with its limitless toll of human agony and social disruption, in the rise of vocational discontent, and in the unconscionably high suicide and homicide rate. Every real redblooded American male should be entitled to carry a six-shooter, shouldn't he? If he shoots sickly, aw shucks! The Mystique's role in the rising divorce rate and the fall of family cohesion and stability, with its wretched social consequences, has already been discussed. An insufficiently appreciated horror of the Mystique is the rigidity its stereotypes impose upon the social corpus. Even a cognizant political personage, or an aware social reformer, experiences difficulty in breaking free from its coercive caricatures. Let's hypothecate the real live Second Coming of Christ, accompanied, hand in hand, by the long-awaited Messiah of the Hebrews. There they stand, in the flesh, on Broadway, the Strand, the Ginza, or Miami Beach; with God overhead, watching for the final deliverance of humankind He had promised eons ago. There is one difficulty, however. Christ is corpulent, and the Hebrew Messiah is heavy-set. Total disaster! Who would believe a rotund savior?! Our agents of salvation must presumably be cast in the heroic mold, either with the musculature of a Michelangelo sculpture or the lean, hard frame popularized by Gary Cooper and other trendsetters of the Mystique. Even our social saviors must fit the mold, or risk being laughed out of town. Is the salvation of humanity worth the expulsion of the Mystique from its earthly paradise? It might appear an eminently sensible and reasonable exchange, even to society.

The sacrifice suffered by the male, were he to turn from his love affair with the Mystique, is realistically negligible. Imitating a satanic pact, which is of highly questionable legality, the Mystique has offered men fantasies and impossible ideals, in exchange for their souls or their humanity. In turning from the Mystique, the male will surrender only anachronistic and meaningless prerogatives. In rejoining the other half of the human race, he may more equitably share the onus, the responsibility, and the work load with his female counterpart. His survival might be enhanced by greater affection and satisfaction from woman, who may become more his partner than his antagonist.

When the Mystique's swan song is finally sung, women stand to gain the rational goals of the Feminist Movement, plus a few additional bonuses. Fulfillment as independent human beings, with increased latitude and opportunity for personal growth and development, would inevitably follow the establishment of a peer relationship with the male. Discrimination against the female by society has always been strongly encouraged and abetted by the Mystique. The departure of the Mystique would remove the *agent provocateur* behind the subjugation of women. No longer inhibited from a free and equal relationship with their lovers and mates, the battle of the sexes would speedily end in an unconditional truce. While this may not exactly return Adam and Eve to their Edenic idyll, it would be a step in the right direction. Women would benefit from the reduced intensity of male exertions as Provider, Achiever, and happy Hero by a diminution in the premature death and disability of their husbands, with couples consequently living longer lives together, marked by less acrimony and greater conjugal activity. Again, the price seems right.

Once the unanimity of the Mystique's defenders has

been shaken, the question arises: How to handily dispose of the Mystique, liberate the male, allow for his humane survival, and perform similar miraculous feats? Turn from overall strategy to tactics. Since strong resistance is anticipated, we should look, not to revolution, which would only tighten the Mystique's defenses, but to evolution, evolution with all deliberate speed. The emphasis by certain elements within the Feminist Movement on immediate and total social revolution proved only counterproductive and alienated many potential allies. Let us learn from their errors and be more limited in aim and more discreet in tactic. By all means, dare to disturb the universe, but do it gently. Don't push for the single, total, immediate and sweeping reform, but attempt a gradual restructuring of the more crucial areas in the society which most urgently press the male. The popularization of passivity as a perfectly reasonable male prerogative might serve as a simple example. There is no commandment that the male must always be the aggressive initiator; why should he not be allowed the occasional role of the passive receptor without loss of his "masculinity"? The escape from that existential vine can best be accomplished by intelligence and poise rather than by a frenzied fumble.

Our tactics would include contact and cooperation with the media, aware of its interest and investment in the newsworthy. A plethora of periodicals, articles, and books on the gut experiences of the male in our society should stimulate both men and women. Borrowing from the Feminist Movement, consciousness-raising sessions should be established in schools, universities, clubs, lodges, and places of business. The intention of these sessions would be the modification of psychological assumptions about men. Masculinity should not automatically be equated with aggression, violence, and cutthroat competitiveness. It is neither biologically inherent in the male (there are gentle societies, albeit in remote and isolated regions), nor socially essential, although our society heavily inculcates its fledgling males with these dubious virtues. How to stop one's son from suffering the same indoctrination might occupy an evening or two, or a decade or two, or a generation. It must be effectuated in the home, in the schools, and in the streets. But what will the consequences be in the tender surroundings of our concrete battlegrounds; would he fare better or worse? Would a disdain for unnecessary violence, assuming the means to defend himself, diminish his probabilities of being attacked, or would it provoke challenge? No one presently knows the answers, but the sessions should not be dull.

This matter of survival, the grist of male emancipation, would be incomplete without at least a potpourri of particulars to be tucked away in the recesses of any male survival kit, ready for more immediate use.

Let us first dispense with the Mystique. The male neophyte should be innoculated against and protected from it. Little boys should be allowed to cry, to express and receive affection and tender feeling, to hug and to kiss. Being naturally human is neither "weakening" nor criminal; the attempt to fashion a rod of steel from young human flesh is. It is long past the time to deemphasize aggressiveness; our society is already supersaturated with its excesses. Children are currently being rewarded for aggressive behavior by parents who approve of winning at any cost. The heroic ideals offered to our offspring are generally victors in violence. Our military and historical heroes, the protagonists of movies and television series, and even the gods taught in mythology classes frequently excel in murder and mayhem. Apparently the human race has fewer built-in inhibitions against killing members of its own species than any other mammal, with the possible exception of the rat. If we continue to reward and idealize aggression and violence, we only encourage and abet a rat-pack mentality which can eventually shorten the survival not only of the male, but of the entire human race. A redefinition of "masculinity" is called for; one which emphasizes intelligence, effectiveness, and understanding, one which extols man's humanitarian virtues rather than his destructive potentials. To facilitate this, movies, television, and the newspapers should be induced to develop heroes who excel in considerate and creative thought and action rather than in brawn and brutality. Let's keep the Neanderthal properly confined, or make of its modern expression a joke and an object of derision. Under the proper circumstances, and appropriately applied, humor can be lethal to the fallacious and the fraudulent. Our new masculine heroes should be those who can rise above the conventional, who view the manifestations of the Mystique, not with contempt, but with pity and understanding, as relics of the past.

The Achiever Complex should be equated with Santayana's definition of fanaticism: "Redoubling your effort when you have forgotten your aim." The man obsessed with achievement should have a reasonable goal in mind. Once this goal is attained, a thoughtful and reflective pause is in order. If he feels impelled to further push on, with no apparent end in view, he should calculate the personal costs involved and perhaps seek psychiatric advice if the price outweighs any reasonable and expectable benefits.

The Sexual Athlete should take a seventh-inning stretch and consider the welfare of his penis. While an increase in the recreational aspects of sexuality is strongly recommended, the relational components should not be negated. "The Sex Life of a Penis" is not to be construed as an invitation to a never-ending and indiscriminate orgy, although no one prefers being the last to arrive at these soirees. In their proper proportion and place, relational considerations enhance sexual satisfaction. A sexual experience should be appreciated, like a fine wine or a good cigar, rather than being regarded as a chore, a test, or an act completely devoid of significance. Chaotic or indiscriminate sexuality is a rather dubious delight. A man related the following incident to me: "I was dining alone at a restaurant. At an adjacent table sat an attractive woman. Naturally, I smiled at her, and was rather pleasantly surprised when she smiled back. I invited her to join me, and she happily obliged. You can imagine my embarrassment when she reminded me that we had slept together only six months ago." Something is clearly out of whack here. There is nothing sacred or holy *about* sex, but there is something intimate and personal *in* sex.

Despite the differences in the physiological sexual capacities between men and women, there exists a basic equality in male and female sexuality which should be accepted by men and women. Women would be wise not to mock the penis. They should recognize the latent fragility of many men, encourage rather than reject, and, by judicious behavior, salvage difficult but potentially rewarding relationships. A single sexual performance is not necessarily a barometer of ability, affection, or concern; it may only be a reflection of anxiety, alcohol, or fatigue.

One medical word of caution. There appears to be a disproportionate number of heart attacks occurring in middle-aged men in hotel and motel rooms in extramarital territory. The anxiety engendered, the pressure of time, the fear of discovery, and the hit-and-miss circumstances may trigger a coronary in those predisposed to develop one. If a man over the age of forty is contemplating such an extramarital liaison, he would be well advised to have a precautionary medical checkup first, including an electrocardiogram. The ever-faithful husband, on the other hand, lying in accustomed arms in the familiar and unpressured surroundings of his bedroom has nothing to fear. The energy expenditure in marital intercourse is the equivalent of climbing two flights of stairs. If a man can do that, he's in. Such are some of the strange and strained circumstances of male survival!

Moving from the more direct expressions of the Mystique to other pressing matters of male survival, the question of life style and philosophy must be considered by the emancipated male.

Man's wonderful workaday world apparently falls short of the ecstatic. The Provider is little more than a beast of burden, for whom life and work are synonymous. This cries out for modification. A man is more than that which he produces, and his vocation should consequently be only a circumscribed area within the totality of his identity. While labor is nothing to be ashamed of, it is by no means a blessing. The puritan work ethic should be removed as the Eleventh Commandment. If a man provides for himself and his family, he is worthy of honor. If he goes beyond, and devotes his life to his work, well, that's his option or his problem, but he deserves no chorus of accolades as a reward. Industry has finally taken notice of vocational discontent on the part of its employees, but is taking remedial measures at the pace of a disabled snail. The human element must invade the industrial complex. Men should adamantly demand and advocate more respect, responsibility, and autonomy at work. Job descriptions can be redesigned to enhance the worker's dignity. If a man's employment is made more interesting, personally rewarding, and stimulating, a decreased sense of alienation will occur within the worker's psyche. Furthermore, the post-retirement depression must be anticipated, and management should provide adequate preparation for it, perhaps as a major function of the Personnel Department. Benjamin Disraeli commented that "Youth is a blunder; manhood a struggle; and old age a regret." Obviously we cannot totally remove remorsefulness from the elderly, but we can modify the vocational aspect of it. Innovations such as paternity leaves, working at home, when feasible, and the staggering of working hours to suit the needs of the individual, where practicable, would reduce the chasm existing between the office and the home, increase family stability, and diminish the split personality of the worker. These are but a few superficial suggestions; how much more can be done to salvage the Provider!

Marriage and family should be freed from society's social imperative. A man should regard marriage as one of several life styles which he is free to choose or to avoid, devoid of social stigma or disapprobation, depending only upon his personal proclivities. He should only marry if he is reasonably comfortable with the idea, and with his prospective spouse. Divorce is emotionally painful and financially costly. A wife should be selected with commonality and compatibility given as much weight as the romantic factor. From its inception, a marriage should be viewed as a lifelong relationship, which should constantly be worked at, with the continual sharing of responsibilities and interests. Children should be regarded as luxuries rather than necessities. By all means conceive them, but only if both partners are willing to make the requisite investment in affection, time, and money. The seventeenth-century Deists postulated a God who created the world, and then left it to spin on its own. One simply cannot do this with children. Once they are created, they require the continued involvement of both parents, very definitely including the interest and concern of their father. If the male is not prepared for so extensive an undertaking, he may be left with a pack of severely troubled children who can prove to be a plague rather than a source of perpetual pleasure. Think twice, or a third time, before making that final insemination.

One final item in the survival kit. A man is first a human being, his maleness or masculinity being only a secondary phenomenon. The emphasis should always devolve on his humanness, with "masculinity" far back in second or third place. As a male, his potentials may be great, but so is his vulnerability. Would that child-rearing techniques followed this thesis! There is a joy in mastery and creativity, but there is also joy in living a full and a satisfactory life, one which, if given the choice, the man would elect to repeat. A satisfactory survival should take precedence over the test of symbolic attainment.

There is a continuum between Camus' "Man must live and create. Live to the point of tears," and Euripides' "Life is a short affair. We should try to make it smooth and free of strife." Each man must find the point between these polarities which best fits his constitution and psychology, and stick to it, despite the pushings and proddings of even the best-intentioned souls within his environmental orbit. There are many versions of Buddha's final words to his disciples. My favorite is: "Seek thy salvation with diligence." What more can each man do?

# Index